The Author, now retired, lives in a Victorian house with a large garden in South Devon. In his professional life, he was a lawyer specialising in planning law. He has always been an active musician, playing keyboards and the flute. His other main interest is astronomy, and he is an honorary life member of the Torbay Astronomical Society, of which he was Secretary for several years.

As a Francophile, he is a student of the French Language and culture, and has visited France many times on holiday, to visit friends there, and on twinning visits.

Best Wish to Joyce

from

Dennis Humphreys

To my dear wife, Liz, who passed away recently, with gratitude for our long and happy life together, including those wonderful visits to France.

Dennis Humphreys

THE CURIOUS TALE OF A FRENCH SALESMAN

AUSTIN MACAULEY PUBLISHERS™

LONDON • CAMBRIDGE • NEW YORK • SHARJAH

A CIP catalogue record for this title is available from the British Library.

ISBN 9781035804894 (Paperback)
ISBN 9781035804900 (ePub e-book)

www.austinmacauley.com

First Published 2023
Austin Macauley Publishers Ltd®
1 Canada Square
Canary Wharf
London
E14 5AA

Thanks to Jacqui, my devoted French teacher, for all her help with the French language and for introducing me to French literature and culture.

Thanks to Judi for her wonderful hospitality in France, and to Liz and Sam for proof reading and suggestions.

Chapter One

Esther was taking a walk from her apartment in Lyon on her way to the local park, her walking stick in her right hand and Fredi's lead in her left hand. Fredi was her rather elderly poodle but still was looking forward to his run in the park. It was late afternoon on a warm day in the spring of 1968, with hawthorn blossom on many of the trees in the park. As always, Esther was smartly dressed, on this occasion in a dark red dress, with a matching summer jacket and a summer hat. Her grey hair was neatly styled, following her visit to her hairdresser, Mme Chantier, earlier in the week.

Esther was a Jewish lady who had lived in Lyon since the end of the Second World War with her daughter-in-law, Martha, and her two grandchildren, Lionel and Rebecca (Martha's children). Esther was a widow, her husband, Jacob Steinfeld, having died at the end of the Great War. Martha was also a widow, as her husband, Joseph, had perished in a Nazi concentration camp in 1943. Neither lady had remarried or had any wish to do. Esther, as a widow with two young sons, was often encouraged to remarry during the period between the world wars, by friends and also by the wider Jewish community. But for Esther, no man could compare with her Jacob, and she could never give her heart to another and so she stayed single and spent her time caring for Joseph and Martha and later for their children, as well.

Esther was well known in the area, each passer-by said, "Good afternoon, Mme Steinfeld."

She gave them a smile and also wished them good afternoon. She hoped that she might meet a friend in the park and have a chat, as she enjoyed the company and sharing news. When she entered the park, she let Fredi off his lead, and he went off exploring the world of smells and sounds, which only dogs understand. As for Esther, she walked beside the lake and was met with a very pleasant surprise: she saw a very old friend, Amelie, whom she had known ever since the time the family moved to Lyon in 1945. Amelie had been in Paris for the last two years, supporting her daughter, Marie-Claire, who had been going through a traumatic divorce with her husband, Rashid. It had originally been a very happy marriage, but in all honesty, both spouses had behaved badly and had at times been unfaithful. Things went really sour.

When they met, Esther said, "How wonderful to see you. It's been so long."

The two ladies embraced and kissed on the cheek in the French style: they took a seat together on a park bench. Fredi saw what was happening and moved over to sit next to the two ladies hoping for a stroke from one of them. Amelie obliged, and said that she was so pleased that her friend still had Fredi.

"How are things in Paris?" Esther asked.

Amelie replied that it was all settled now: the couple were still on bad terms with each other but the issues about the apartment, the business and everything else had been resolved, thanks in part to some very sensible lawyers on both sides.

"How about the children?"

"Well they are twenty and eighteen and both are at the Sorbonne. There is joint custody but the kids are virtually independent anyway. They seem to dislike both parents in equal measure. Incidentally, they spend more time in demonstrations than studying as far as I can gather. I feel annoyed about that, because some of us did not have the benefit of a university education, and they should make the most of it."

"I entirely agree. It is a privilege to have higher education. There seem to be demonstrations all over the country. What is the matter with people? They seem to be rejecting everything their parents have taught them."

"How have you been?" asked Amelie.

"Well, I am afraid that my heart condition has got worse. I saw the consultant last week, and there is no more that they can do for me at my age. I am continuing on the same medication and advised to rest and take regular gentle exercise, which is what I do. I am trying my best to avoid another heart attack. The consultant rules out an operation. But how is your health?"

"I have been clear of cancer for seven years, and hopefully it will stay that way."

"I hope so too. Where are you living now?"

"We are renting a lovely apartment in the Rue Rambert."

"That's very near us. We are still in the block over there. You must come and have a meal with us. Martha cooks well. It's mainly kosher but always tastes really good."

"Albert and I would like that very much. Incidentally, I saw your grandson in the city centre the other day. Quite the smart businessman, in a nice suit and with a briefcase, getting into a swish silver car, a Citroën, I think. So different from the shy young lad which I knew when you first moved here, after the war. Is he still single? If so, he would be quite a catch for some girl."

"Despite his looks, Lionel is still quite shy, especially with girls. At twenty-eight, he ought at least to have a girlfriend. Anyway, that's what a Jewish grandmother thinks, but it's entirely up to him. Martha was worried that he might be one of those homos but I don't believe that. He looks so much like my dear Jacob. Strong build, good posture, and handsome, at least in my opinion. The only difference is that he has fair hair, while Jacob was dark-haired."

"What does he do?"

"Since he left school, it must be ten years ago, he has worked for Mallet Frères, who sell electrical stuff all around the country. He is now amazingly one of their top salesmen, hence the smart car and suit."

"How does he manage if he is still shy?"

"Well, I am not sure but he absolutely loves the electrical goods and all the modern gadgets, and seems to lose all self-consciousness when talking about them to anyone. He is a round peg in a round hole."

"That's great."

"I must go now, my dear, as Martha will be home soon from the lycée, and she may need help with dinner. Here's our phone number."

"Thanks and here's ours. It was so wonderful to meet up with you."

The ladies embraced and Esther and Fredi made their way home, neither moving as fast as they had in the past.

Chapter Two

Esther went back to the apartment and awaited Martha's return from the lycée. Martha came home quite late carrying a large briefcase full of homework to mark. She looked tired and Esther was a little concerned.

"You look a little tired, dear. Shall I get us something to eat tonight? I expect Lionel will be home by eight o'clock and I can get things done by then."

"If you could, that would really help. It was a hard day as we have been getting ready for the inspectors, who are due next week. The principal went through everything with a toothcomb and there were so many forms to fill up. In addition, I had the usual workload of teaching. We are working the classes hard now with exams coming up."

Esther got ready to prepare an evening meal.

Then Lionel arrived home. Unlike his mother, he looked very fresh and full of energy and talked to Martha and Esther about his exciting day in the electrical goods business. They were interested mainly because it was Lionel who was telling the story, otherwise, they might have been a little bored.

At about eight o'clock, the three of them sat down for the food which Esther had prepared. Lots of fresh salads and vegetables, with herbs and spices and a little pan-fried veal.

This was followed by a French-type fruit tart from the local boulangerie. They drank fruit juice or spring water, as they rarely consumed alcohol.

They talked as they enjoyed their meal. Esther told them her news, "I had a pleasant surprise on my visit to the park. I met Amelie there by chance. They are now back in Lyon, living in the Rue Rambert. Their daughter's divorce has been resolved, so they are able to come back here. It would be nice to have them over for a meal."

The others agreed. Martha added that she would prefer a weekend when she might be less tired.

Esther interjected that it would be nice if it were a weekend when Rebecca would be home. Again, they agreed.

Esther and Martha talked about their recent time at the synagogue, which they visited regularly partly to pray for Jacob and Joseph but also for Lionel and Rebecca. Lionel looked slightly embarrassed as he rarely attended with them.

He was not a religious person, although he greatly respected his mother and grandmother, to whom he owed so much. He was certainly not an atheist but perhaps an agnostic. He was a great admirer of the modern secular state, which was France. There had been much economic growth in the country during his life-time, and he liked all the modern artefacts which were then available. He loved the goods which the company sold, especially the labour-saving devices which made people's lives easier, and the clever new products which increased the quality of life for his customers.

In his job as a commercial traveller for Mallet Frères, his work took him to various parts of France to advertise his company's goods and obtain orders.

Lionel then talked about his day. He was very proud to say that his manager, M. Dupont, was delighted with his recent business trips and had told him that for his next trip he could go away for a whole week to whatever part of France he might choose.

Lionel told the ladies all about this and suggested where he might go.

"I was thinking of going to the Auvergne or to the far southwest near the Pyrenees. I vaguely remember the Auvergne from when I was very young and I have always wanted to see the Pyrenees and the historic towns in that region, like Beziers and Carcassonne."

Martha responded, "I have rather sad memories of our difficult time in the Auvergne during the War. But I do not think that either of the regions you have in mind are particularly prosperous. You have not yet tried your luck in northern France, where there is apparently a higher standard of living and maybe more demand for up-to-date household products. This includes the Paris region but also Normandy and Brittany."

"I ruled out that part of France as Paris has a strong commercial interest there and I would be competing head-on with Paris-based companies. I might be knocking my head against a brick wall."

Then Esther had a strong feeling from somewhere deep inside her that Lionel should definitely go to northeast France. She proposed, "I would suggest that you try northeast France near to Belgium, which I believe is up and coming. You could even cross the border into Belgium, which is now in the Common Market, and where French is spoken."

Lionel thought for a moment, and pondered, ending up to his surprise finding the idea rather appealing. He knew nothing of the area, and it would be a real adventure going there.

He replied, "It would involve a very long car journey, but there is a place where I could stop off on the way to stay with a work colleague. I have also been allocated a new company car, a large silver Citroën, which is great to drive. I will need to clear it with my boss, but I expect him to approve."

After the meal, Martha went into her study to do her marking and did not finish until eleven o'clock, by which time Esther had gone to bed.

While Martha was doing her marking, Lionel and Esther were studying maps of the proposed area of France. They also found a guidebook, which was rather out of date, but still quite useful.

Esther suggested, "St Auban looks like a good starting point in that region. It's a sizeable town near the Belgian border and would surely have plenty of shops and other businesses, plus places to stay for a few nights."

Lionel was impressed with his grandmother's analysis and added, "It even has a cathedral so it must be a city. Maybe there are facilities connected with the church, which might like to have some of my products! Monks must cook and clean sometimes."

Esther laughed and Lionel set his heart on going to that area to try his luck there.

That night, Esther had a repeat of a dream that she had had the previous night. In it, she was with Lionel and suddenly they were joined by her late husband, Jacob, still a young man in the dream. She noticed how similar in looks he was to

17

Lionel, except for the hair colour. Jacob just smiled and then vanished, leaving Esther and Lionel feeling confused.

Chapter Three

The family were comfortably off now. Lionel had his salary and bonuses from his work and, for some years, Martha had taught English in a lycée in the city. His younger sister, Rebecca, came home sometimes and was a trainee engineer with an aerospace company in Toulouse. Their apartment was in a smart part of Lyon, not far from the Rhone. They could afford to dress well and to take an annual holiday on the South Coast. Martha could afford to run a car, and Lionel had a Citroen 2CV to get him to and from work when a company car was not available.

Life had not always been anywhere near so comfortable for them, both during the Second World War and as from 1945, when they moved to Lyon. Esther vividly recalled their early years in Lyon. She well remembered how in September 1945, she stood at a school entrance with five-year-old Lionel awaiting his first day at school. He was rather thin and shabbily dressed, with an apprehensive look on his face. At the time, the family was living in a down-at-heel tenement block in the city, which was all they could afford.

Lionel's late father, Joseph, had been an outspoken journalist and was unable to join the army in 1939 on account of an injury to his leg in an earlier industrial accident. He had been vociferous in his criticism of the French government and of the Nazi regime. He had even been bold enough to criticise Marshal Pétain, now in charge of the Vichy Government. This had made him many influential enemies. In 1943, he ended up being denounced as a Jew and handed over to the Nazis. He was placed in a concentration camp in Germany and was shot and killed on trying to escape along with other prisoners. This was brave on his part but rather rash as he was disabled. After his arrest, the family, fearing for their safety, fled to a remote part of the Auvergne, where some second cousins lived. They left Clermont in a hurry and lost most of their assets. With aid of the French Resistance based at Aurillac, the family was kept hidden in a remote farmhouse, receiving some help from the Resistance and some from a nearby Jewish community. But they were poor and life was very difficult for them: Esther, Martha, Lionel and little sister Rebecca, who was only one year old. This vast and beautiful area could be very hot in summer, but bitterly cold in winter. Often, they struggled to find enough firewood to keep themselves warm.

When the war ended and it was safe for them to come out, they relocated to Lyon, where again they had some distant relatives. They could only afford to rent a cheap apartment. Esther looked after the home and cared for the children, whilst Martha took badly paid jobs in shops and cafes to provide some income for the family. They received a little help from the synagogue. After a few years and long hours of study, Martha qualified as a teacher and got a post as an English teacher in a lycée, which meant that the life of the family improved substantially. Eventually, they could move to a much better apartment where they still remained.

At first, school was difficult for Lionel, as some pupils constantly bullied him, because he was different, being from an underprivileged household, without a father and Jewish. He did not, therefore, do well at school in his early years but his mother taught him at home to read, write and do arithmetic, and he became competent at all three, which stood him in good stead in later life.

He always remembered one day when, as he was leaving school a little late with no staff about, he was set upon by two bullies.

"Let's beat up this smelly Jew. All Jews are scum and traitors to France."

They pushed Lionel over and started to kick him on the ground. He covered his face with his hands to protect himself as well as he could. When he was expecting serious injury, suddenly unexpected help arrived in the form of Marcel Novak, a young Romani boy, whose family had settled in Lyon in a permanent Gipsy camp. The young Marcel assisted his father at weekends with his scrap metal business, and thereby became extremely strong for his age as a result of lifting heavy weights.

Marcel seeing what was happening, shouted, "Leave him alone, you scum bags!"

The two bullies left Lionel on the ground and turned their attention to Marcel.

"Well, well, we have a filthy Gipsy here, perhaps he wants to be beaten up."

With that, one of them took a swing at Marcel, which he easily parried. Marcel, thinking quickly, decided not to hit him with full force as it would have broken his jaw. Instead, he struck him on the chin hard enough to knock him to the ground. The other bully, who was older, then had a go, but Marcel picked him up bodily and threw him into a ditch.

The two bullies crawled away. Marcel reckoned that there would be no more trouble from them, as they would not wish to admit that they had been beaten up by a young Gipsy boy. Not much later, they were expelled from school following an aggravated assault in the town and also were in serious trouble with the police.

Lionel went over to Marcel and thanked him for what he had done.

Marcel said, "That's okay. Jews and Gipsies are minorities who get blamed for things and get picked on. I have always tried to defend myself. You look like quite a strong guy. You should learn how to fight, and to sort the scum out."

Lionel and Marcel became great friends, and Lionel occasionally used to visit the Gipsy encampment to meet Marcel's family.

As Lionel got older, there was a big change: he had grown in height and developed considerable physical strength. No more bullying thereafter. He was not, however, academically gifted but showed real skill at sports, especially football and tennis. He was selected for the lycée's football team when only sixteen – good for his self-confidence and for his image with others, especially as he scored goals.

There was, however, tragic news for him at this impressionable stage in his life. His friend Marcel was diagnosed with a rare and incurable form of leukaemia and sadly died shortly afterwards. Lionel was inconsolably sad and was allowed to attend the funeral, the only non-Gipsy there. Marcel's parents were very moved by Lionel's presence, and afterwards, he visited them regularly, to let them know how much he loved and respected Marcel and how much he missed him. Lionel and Marcel's family became friends. Esher and Martha knew that this was happening and kept an open mind about it. Gipsies did not have a good reputation at that time in the city. Whilst they did not want to stop the relationship with Marcel's parents, they did not want to give much encouragement either.

One day, when he went to see them after school, Marcel's dad, Pavel, said to him, "Lionel my dear boy, we have a special visitor today, who would like to meet you. She is Aunt Rose, a very famous fortune-teller. If you would like, she will tell your fortune!"

Lionel, although thoroughly sceptical about fortune-telling and astrology, decided to meet her, partly from a desire to be polite but also from pure curiosity. As she was called, "Aunt", he assumed that she must be of the generation older than Marcel's parents, maybe as old as his grandmother. Marcel's mum then took Lionel to a large and impressive caravan, with a sign on it, "Aunt Rose Fortune-Teller".

Marcel's mum left and Lionel rather tentatively entered the caravan. He was very surprised at the sight of Aunt Rose. She was much younger than he had been expecting and stunningly beautiful in an exotic way. She was in her late thirties, tall with long black hair, with a natural wave in it and pinned back from her face with jewelled hair clips. She was wearing a full-length black cotton dress, with its hem cut diagonally revealing a red cotton underskirt. She wore a beautiful red shawl, trimmed with lace, around her shoulders, and a black choker decorated with jewels around her neck. She wore long silver earrings. She had hypnotic dark brown eyes and was wearing a little mascara and a hint of lipstick.

Her nail varnish was a dark red, and she was wearing silver bracelets.

She spoke in a soft and mellow voice, and in a foreign accent that he could not quite place, "Welcome, Lionel. I have heard a lot about you. How kind you are and how you are a real friend of the Romani people."

"Would you like Aunt Rose to tell you your fortune?"

Lionel noticed a sign about her charges and enquired how much it would cost?

"There is no charge for a friend of the family, but be aware that I will tell you what I see whether it is good or not so good."

Lionel agreed to proceed. His head told him that this was just mumbo-jumbo, but he was mesmerised by Aunt Rose, and his heart was telling him that she could look into his very soul and know everything that had happened to him and what would happen in the future.

She looked intently into his eyes and then took his hands, one at a time to look at his palms. He felt a thrill at the touch of her long, elegant hands on his. Then she said that she would like to touch his head, and he nodded his assent. She put her hands over his temples and then gradually on the rest of his head. Immediately afterwards, she placed her hands on her crystal ball in stages exactly as they had been on his head. She gazed at the crystal ball and spoke quietly but with real authority,

"I see a beautiful young lady with dark hair and brown eyes. She is smartly dressed and she is elegant and graceful. A young man comes close to her. He has fair hair, it is you Lionel. The couple embrace and fall in love. But I see clouds overhead. There are problems but in the end, they are overcome and the young couple marry and have a long and happy life together. I can also see that you are a person of great integrity, who can be trusted. You will always do well in your career whatever it may be. You have a very bright future to look forward to."

Lionel was dumbfounded and did not know what to think or say.

After a pause, he asked tentatively and politely, "Is the young lady a beautiful Romani lady, like you, Aunt Rose?"

Aunt Rose wondered if this nice young man was seeking to flirt with her. She was mildly amused but concluded that he was asking a genuine and direct question, with no other agenda.

She responded, "She might be Romani or perhaps a lady from Spain, southern France or Italy, the countries near the Mediterranean."

Naively, he enquired whether he should go to those countries to find her.

"No, it would be too difficult as there would be so many lovely young women in all those countries. No need to go there. It is your fortune to meet her wherever that may happen. Remember, people travel about. You may even meet here in Lyon, or in Vienna, where I often stay, or in Berlin, Paris or Marseille."

Lionel thanked her in words which he found hard to articulate and left her caravan. He could never forget what this amazing lady had told him. He hoped it might one day all come true.

When Lionel had not returned home at the expected time, his mother had become anxious. She was aware that he was to visit the Gipsy Site after school, but normally he was back home earlier on the days when he made those visits. She hoped he had not been assaulted, as on that horrible day when he had been attacked on leaving school. When he got back home, she said, "You are a bit later than we were expecting. Was everything okay?"

"Yes. We just talked a bit longer than usual, and I lost track of time."

He did not mention Aunt Rose and the prediction for his fortune. He suspected that Martha and Esther would not have approved, as they would not have believed in astrology or fortune-telling, being contrary to their deeply held religious views.

That weekend, Amelie and Albert came over for a meal with them, and Rebecca joined them. It was a very happy occasion, except when Amelie kept asking Lionel about girlfriends, and when Albert expressed the view that increased crime in the city was due to Gipsies in the area. He was also surprised that girls could do engineering. Lionel did not show any reaction to the questions posed or the comments made. He had to bite his tongue. Rebecca took no notice, as she knew that she was an excellent engineer and was a lot brighter than Albert. The conversation moved on to other subjects, such as the university protests and government policy.

When the guests had departed, Lionel said to his mother, "Please warn me when they are coming again so that I can arrange to be at the cinema with my mates."

She knew exactly what he meant.

Chapter Four

The sequence of events which led to Lionel becoming a travelling salesman began when he reached the age of eighteen and was due to leave the lycée.

He had a long discussion with his mother as to whether he should seek to go into higher or further education of some kind. He had not done well academically at school but was literate and numerate to a good standard. He could have thought of studying law or accountancy, but he did not want to go to a school or college of any kind. He wanted a job and to earn money in the real world. He was aware of how poor they had been during his young years and had a strong desire always to earn an income and pay his way, and, if necessary, take care of the family. This was a mature attitude for an eighteen-year-old, but that was what he was like.

With some reluctance, his mother was persuaded that university or higher education was not for him and that he should try his luck in the job market. She thought how different her two children were: Rebecca was so good at maths and science and also very confident and ambitious, whereas Lionel was less talented but also tended to undervalue himself. There was, however, an underlying determination to succeed. In a few years, her young daughter would become a fully qualified engineer with Airbus at Toulouse, and later help design space rockets at NASA.

Lionel found a job at Mallet Frères as a warehouseman in a depot of a company formed in the 1950s, but which had expanded considerably in the 1960s with increased prosperity in France and new products coming on to the market. The company manufactured and imported household electrical goods: fridges, freezers, vacuum cleaners and smaller kitchen gadgets. Lionel intended that this should be a temporary job while he looked around for other opportunities and also gained experience in the workplace. He was just an odd job man there, but an exceptionally good one. His inner determination and enthusiasm were soon recognised by the depot manager.

As a physically strong young man, he soon found that he loved his work, including loading and unloading lorries and vans. The young women in the depot were impressed with him, but he never really noticed. He also loved the new products and all aspects of modernity. He made himself familiar with the products, their design and function and how to operate them. Sometimes he would say to his immediate boss at the depot that an instruction manual was inaccurate or misleading, particularly those translated badly from Italian or German. This impressed his boss and led him to make changes to address the problem which Lionel had found. It became obvious to the company that, although Lionel did not have any great qualifications, he had practical skills plus business acumen.

As for leisure activities, after leaving school, he gave up football but continued playing tennis. He joined a tennis club near their home, and much enjoyed playing the game, at which he was very talented. At the club, he met lots of girls and young women, but although he found them attractive, he was very shy and ill at ease in their company. He enjoyed playing mixed doubles but made a point of not using his fastest service to a female opponent. This sometimes displeased his partner at the time, who did not enjoy the same help from the other male player in the match. He was far too shy to chat up the younger women. Some of the older ones found him dishy and flirted with him, but that just made him feel embarrassed. Although he had plenty of opportunities to meet girls and was quite attractive to some of them, he never managed to have a girlfriend at Lyon. This became a continuing disappointment to him, especially when he saw his mates in happy relationships. *What's the matter with me?* he thought.

He also retained somewhere in the back of his mind the thought that his true love would be a girl with dark hair and brown eyes. Most of the ladies at the club were blonde, natural or otherwise.

As a result of his excellent work in the depot, Lionel had been appointed as a commercial traveller at the early age of twenty-one. His job was to travel around the country and obtain orders for the company's products. He was given contact details for shops and warehouses, which might want the products. He visited all those potential customers but also, unlike other salesmen, was proactive. He went to public reference libraries, information centres, town halls and chambers of commerce to find out information about businesses and institutions in the region where he might be able to obtain orders, including colleges, schools, hospitals and even prisons.

The result of his efforts was that his trips produced far more orders than those of his colleagues. He was on the way up in his career.

Chapter Five

So it was that in the spring of 1968, after heeding the advice of Esther, his grandmother, that he made his journey to northeast France and arrived at St Auban, which they had selected after careful research. He parked his Citroën in the main square. Those were the days when there were less cars on the road and when one could drive into a town centre and park without difficulty and free of charge. As expected, he found the town hall there. He guessed correctly that the public library would be close by, which it was. One entered the library via the town hall, which Lionel then did, arriving there at about a quarter to five. He would have liked to have arrived earlier, but he had been held up by roadworks and also a major accident on the highway.

At the reception desk, he asked a librarian politely for some information about businesses in the area. Her response, (a middle-aged woman of forbidding aspect), was unhelpful and abrupt.

"We are closing at five o'clock and anyway I have a lot of admin to do in my office. You will have to come back tomorrow: we open to the public at 10.00 am."

She pronounced the word, "public" as if it portrayed something unsavoury and irritating.

With that, she left at a speed greater than he thought she was capable. Lionel was surprised and disappointed, as he was hoping to make progress that evening, and to make an early start on his business in the morning.

But there was an assistant still at reception. She appeared to be a young woman: she was wearing a head scarf, with reading glasses and dressed in an ill-fitting greyish uniform which was too large for her. Her face looked pallid and depressed under the fluorescent lights of the library. She was sorting out a huge pile of index cards. Putting them aside, she spoke to him quietly and politely.

"I can stay for half an hour, sir, as my bus does not leave until five-thirty. What sort of information were you looking for?"

He explained and she immediately understood what he wanted. She was amazingly helpful and courteous and in no time found for him gazetteers, trade directories, telephone books, tourist information and maps. She helped and guided him to find useful entries and obviously knew the area very well. He was truly grateful and delighted, as he had found a wealth of very useful information. He wrote down key points very carefully in his note-book in his usual copperplate handwriting, as was his custom on these occasions.

He said to the young assistant, in obviously appreciative tones, "You have been very helpful, miss, and the information is invaluable. I'd like to stay in the area for a few days. I was wondering if there is a good hotel or guest house nearby but not too expensive?"

"Yes, sir, there is. The Hotel du Centre at Moulins. My father is the proprietor. It's not that expensive. The rooms are comfortable and the food is traditional but very good. There should be room vacancies at this time of year. The restaurant will be very busy, as it always is, but some tables are always kept for residents."

"Is that the village about ten kilometres south of here?"

"Yes, that's it."

"I noticed it as I was driving here, but I think there was a bypass."

Then he noticed that she was looking a little anxious and checking her watch. She said, "Oh dear. It is after half-past five and I have missed the bus. I need to get to the hotel right away, as I am needed to help in the restaurant this evening. The head waiter's wife has been taken ill, and he has had to go home."

"I could take you there in my car, which is parked out there in the main square. My name by the way is Lionel Steinfeld and I am from Lyon, where I live with my mother and grandmother."

"Pleased to meet you, M. Steinfeld. I am Marielle Leclerc, and I live in the hotel in our private apartment."

Marielle was reluctant to accept a lift from a man she did not know and was also concerned as to what her dad would say if he found out. She also looked closely at Lionel and saw that he was very smartly dressed and looked really respectable. She was in two minds but, after some thought, responded, "That is a very kind offer, sir, but I will phone Mum who will send Charles over for me."

Lionel sensed why she had turned down his offer and respected her discretion. He set off for Moulins and soon arrived at the hotel, where he parked the car near the entrance of the imposing building. He entered and checked in. He could not help noticing that the hotel was smart: the lady at reception was wearing an elegant blue suit and, as he glanced into the restaurant, he saw that the tables had all been dressed tastefully and properly. This was obviously a place where he needed to wear his best suit and his best silk tie. He hoped it would not be too expensive. Similar hotels near his home would have been well out of his price range.

All the rooms were double. He was shown up to a spacious room at the front of the hotel. There was a large old-style double bed, a large wardrobe, two easy chairs, a desk and chair, a washbasin and a bidet. The room was not ensuite (which was not common at that time) but the bathroom and toilet were next to the room in the corridor. He looked out of the window, wondering if there would be traffic noise. He was assured that, since the bypass was built five years ago, there was little traffic passing through the village, especially at night.

The room was at a very reasonable price and he booked in for six nights. He also booked in for dinner at 7.30 that evening. He took a bath and changed into his smartest clothes, including the silk tie, which Esther had given him for his birthday and which he had not previously worn. He had good feelings about this place: the helpful young lady in the reference library, the unexpectedly nice hotel and something about the area which seemed to him strangely familiar.

Chapter Six

The hotel was owned and managed by a husband-and-wife team, Gaston and Sandrine Leclerc, who had met at Marseille during the war, and relocated to Moulins in 1945, after the hostilities had ceased.

It was in June 1940 that Gaston, a soldier aged twenty-four and from a military family, dressed in civilian clothes, left Paris on one of the last trains to Marseille. The Germans had entered Paris, and France was on the point of surrendering. Gaston, from a French military family, could not stand the sight of German soldiers in the city. He decided to leave his regiment and join a resistance group in Marseille. The train departed in the evening from the Gare de Lyon completely full of passengers escaping from Paris occupied by the enemy.

At Marseille, Gaston found employment in hotels and restaurants, and at the same time, he was helping persons in danger to escape to North Africa, especially Morocco. In a hotel where he was working near the end of the war, he met Sandrine, the owner's beautiful daughter. She was nineteen and had the typical looks of a girl from the Mediterranean region, dark hair and lovely brown eyes. These features she had inherited from her mother who was Spanish. They fell in love and got married in 1944. They lived in an apartment near the harbour and had their first children whilst living there.

Eventually, they had three children, all girls. There were the twin girls born in Marseille and then Marielle, who was born in Moulins in 1946. When Gaston learned that the third child was another girl, he was disappointed, as he was longing for a boy, who could share his interests: the army, rifles, hunting, fishing and fast cars.

Sadly, Gaston never showed any obvious affection for Marielle: he just seemed indifferent to her. It was only with outside activities and sports that they spent much time together. As she was growing up, she always tried to please her father, but without obvious success. However, she grew up to be a considerate and helpful person. She was very close to her mother, who loved her dearly, perhaps making up for her father's indifference. Her father was, however, protective of her as she grew older, as she was the youngest in the family and far less street-wise it seemed than her twin sisters.

He had to sort out a tennis coach who was showing too much interest in her when she was at school. He did not like either of her boyfriends, who wore scruffy jeans and had long hair. He had heard that one of them used cannabis, of which he strongly disapproved.

When the war was over, the family had moved to Moulins, where Marielle was born, a village near the Belgian border, also situated in a region where Gaston's parents lived. In the village, Gaston and Sandrine bought the Hotel de la Gare, a rundown building occupied by the Germans during the war. They had a lot of help, including financial, from Gaston's parents. Having restored it as a hotel, they changed its name to Hotel du Centre. (There was no longer a railway in the village).

Gaston and Sandrine worked very hard indeed: he was a good manager and business man; she was a fine cook. Most days Gaston paid a visit to the food market at St Auban to obtain excellent fresh local produce for the hotel: everything from seafood to game, cheeses and local vegetables. Gaston managed the hotel with military precision: every member of the team had a precise understanding of their role and respected him as a good leader. The hotel was a real success.

When she was eighteen, Marielle got a job in St Auban and also helped at times in the hotel, especially to cover for an absence by a member of staff.

Gaston was a man of good character and well respected in the area, but he had one very serious fault. Although not fanatically anti-Semitic, he disliked the Jews as a result of his family history. His grandfather had been an officer in the military at the time of the notorious Dreyfus affair and he and his family always believed that Dreyfus was guilty of espionage despite overwhelming proof to the contrary. Gaston and his father never believed that Jews were truly faithful to the republic. They also resented the wealth of many Jewish families and felt that they had too much influence.

One of Marielle's twin sisters was Stephanie. In 1968, she was in a relationship with Pierre, who described himself as an entrepreneur. He was a likeable rogue, but Gaston thought of him as a spiv. Gaston was not wrong.

I would not buy a used car or anything else from that chap, he thought.

Stephanie helped Pierre in his dubious ventures and Gaston sincerely hoped that she would not end up in jail.

Neither Stephanie nor the other twin sister, Véronique, had ever paid much regard to their parents' opinions or wishes, and during their youth, they were not supportive of Marielle, whom they regarded as Mummy's pet.

Marielle was completely different: amiable, helpful, obedient and respectful, always wishing to please.

In later years, however, Marielle and Véronique became close friends.

Chapter Seven

Returning to the events in May 1968, on that evening at the hotel, Lionel, having changed in his room and looking really smart, went down to the restaurant. He was seated at a table at one end of the restaurant when Marielle came in. He hardly recognised her, dressed in the traditional style of a French waitress. She was wearing a black three-quarter-length silk dress and a long crisp white apron, edged with lace. The dress fitted her perfectly showing off her shapely figure and he thought the dress must have been made to measure. Her hair was nicely styled and she wore pretty long silver earrings. Her mother had skilfully applied a little make-up to her face. He thought she looked fabulous, which she did.

What a difference from the young lady in that turgid grey outfit in the library.

He saw that she was a very capable waitress, and how with minimum effort she kept all the customers in the busy restaurant happy. She was also clearly the person in charge, as the younger waiting staff all looked to her for guidance at times. As she took his order, he could not take his eyes off her. A young waitress brought him his first course: then as Marielle passed by, she said to him softly, "Bon appétit, monsieur."

His heart skipped a beat at the gentle sound of her voice.

The first course was Salade de Gesier, one of his favourites. It was excellent, beautifully cooked and with wonderful dressing, as was the main course, escalope of veal in a cream and brandy sauce and local new potatoes, the dessert was a superb raspberry soufflé.

Lionel did not drink alcohol and so chose Badoit to accompany his meal. He also had a short strong coffee at the end of the meal. After the first course, he was served by a skilled young waiter of less than twenty years old, who seemed to have a massive crush on Marielle. Lionel was vaguely amused.

At one stage, Marielle came over to his part of the restaurant to reach for a bottle of red wine high up on a rack. As she did so, her skirt rode up a little, revealing the fine white lace at the hem of her petticoat. She became more and more attractive to him.

After the excellent meal, as he was tired and had a busy day ahead of him, he went up to his room before ten o'clock. Marielle was at the other end of the restaurant, and they were not able to exchange words before he retired.

In his room, he undressed and folded up his clothes with care, hanging up his suit in the large wardrobe. He washed, brushed his teeth and got into bed. As usual, he read his newspaper but could not give it his usual concentration. As he lay in bed, he could not help thinking of this lovely girl: intelligent, knowledgeable, delightful, helpful and very stylish. He knew he had always been painfully shy with girls, which he could not really understand, as he was very confident in all his business dealings with men or women. Despite his fears, he decided to ask her for a date and really hoped it would work out for him and that he would not mess up. Sadly, he did not live in the area and he would have to make the most of his time there if he was both to do business and also date this lovely girl.

Marielle did not get to bed until after eleven-thirty, as it had been a busy session in the restaurant, with much clearing up to do. As she lay in bed, she thought about this unusual young man in the library and then at the hotel. He really had something about him. Very smartly dressed. That suit was tailor-made and expensive. He was so devoted to his work and had such good manners. His fair hair was short and tidy, unlike so many of the young men in the area, who had long hair and wore scruffy jeans. He seemed a little formal and aloof but was very appreciative of the help he gave her. She noticed the admiring looks he was giving her in the restaurant. She also thought about his powerful sleek Citroën. She could not get him out of her mind, but being tired she soon fell asleep.

For the next few days, Lionel did not see Marielle, as she was at work in St Auban and he was out on business, not getting back to the hotel until late. He was unaware that Marielle had also been on a training course at Strasbourg during that week. He thought to himself, *Yet again, business has got in the way of my chance of romance. I shall end up a sad old bachelor.*

Chapter Eight

As he was leaving the hotel on the Sunday and taking his bags and paraphernalia to the car, he had some unexpected help from Lady Luck. Marielle happened to be sitting in the garden, reading a magazine. As she saw him, she gave him a warm smile and asked if he was on his way and whether he had had a good business trip. He said he would be leaving soon and that he had had an excellent trip, thanks to all the information she had found for him.

He said that he had decided to take a walk in the local park before setting off and asked her if she would like to join him. To his surprise, she said that she would. She was meeting her sister, Véronique, for lunch at St Auban, but her bus did not go until 12.30. She added that there were few buses on a Sunday. He felt overwhelmingly excited and could not believe his luck. He was also nervous and worried about saying the wrong thing.

They left the hotel together and walked over to the park, in lovely weather, with trees in blossom all around. The situation was perfect. What could go wrong?

Although Lionel was apprehensive and ill at ease, he was at the same time excited to be with Marielle, whom he found so very attractive. He was rather absorbed with his own feelings and did not notice the way she was looking at him, which to a keen observer might have betrayed the fact that she really liked him (or even more).

She was wearing a pretty summer dress, in subtle pastille colours. It was in an old-fashion style with a fairly long skirt, which he found very feminine and stylish. It also showed off her shapely figure.

Instinctively, he said, "Marielle, I really like your dress, it is so beautiful." (A good start.)

"Thank you. I am pleased with it. It is in the 1940s' style and I made it myself from a pattern book."

"That's very impressive. Both my mother and grandmother are good at dressmaking, and I am sure that they would like it." (Maybe not so good: keep Mum out of it.)

Despite his reticence, he did not find it as hard as expected to chat with her. She was very relaxed and cheerful and seemed interested in all he had to say.

They talked about all sorts of things, including the library and her colleague there. Marielle explained, "Aléanor is very well qualified but does not seem to like people or books."

This amused Lionel so much, and despite his shyness, he could not stop laughing. Jokingly, he asked whether Marielle had similar views to her colleague, and she replied that she loved finding information and helping people. There was rarely a customer that she did not like, even commercial travellers. She gave him a knowing smile as she made that teasing remark.

He could not help smiling back at her and then he commented on her rather dull outfit in the library.

She replied, "Normally, I work in Tourist Information, where we have a smart office and modern blue uniforms. Our office is having a refit before the summer season and also because it will be the fiftieth anniversary of the end of the First World War. We are expecting an influx of visitors to the area, because of the history of the area in the Great War. I was asked to help out in the library where they are doing a stocktaking and clearing out a huge number of old books. I was helping to move out old books and to deal with the classification of new ones. That was why they had provided the grey overalls and a headscarf, because of dust, and also why I had to wade through old index cards."

They talked about school, where neither of them had done well. They had both excelled in tennis at school and still played to a good standard.

Lionel commented, "My main weapon on the tennis court is my fast service, which opponents find hard to return. I do not use my fast first serve against female opponents when we play mixed doubles."

"How does your partner feel about that if you go on to lose the point? As an experienced player, I can return most services from any player, except perhaps the real professionals. As a junior, I played at a regional level and got used to all sorts of serves, fast and sliced."

"I would be upset if I hit a lady opponent and caused an injury."

"That's a considerate attitude but club players who regularly play mixed doubles get used to fast serves, and, if they cannot return them, at least know how to get out of the way of the ball."

They talked about music. Marielle asked him what sort of music he listened to. He replied, "I am not keen on American or English pop music but I really enjoy French songs, plus some folk and country music. This is what I listen to in the car. At home, we listen to some classical music and also some traditional Jewish music."

"I don't like pop music, except to dance to. Like you, I much prefer French singers, as well as folk and country, which seem to have a real message you can relate to. Most pop music is just bubble-gum."

Then Marielle changed the subject.

"You mentioned that you live in Lyon, that's a place I have never been to, and I think you said you live with your mother and grandmother. Do you have a girlfriend or anything?"

"I was brought up by my mother and grandmother, as my dad was arrested in the war and deported to Germany, where he was killed in a concentration camp. We had to hide away in the countryside, until 1945, when we relocated to Lyon. There is also my younger sister, Rebecca, who is now a trainee in Toulouse. We were very poor at first but are okay now ever since Mum got a job teaching English in the lycée and of course, I am now in work.

"I am afraid it is all work and no play for me these days and I do not have a girlfriend."

Marielle felt genuinely sorry for him and responded in a sympathetic tone, "It sounds as if you have had a hard life, and I am very sorry about the loss of your father. I guess it was tough for you at times."

"Yes, but my mum and grandma are very strong and wonderful people. They are good at most things including sewing, cooking and making do. We have always eaten well even when money was short.

"The food at your hotel is exquisite. Just the sort of things I like."

"I am pleased that you like it. My parents have always worked very hard and tried to produce good meals from local produce."

It was fortunate that they both loved good food. They had a short chat about dishes and recipes. Lionel felt relaxed and thought they were on the same wavelength.

He noticed how gracefully and elegantly Marielle moved. Aware that she played tennis to a high standard, he felt that she had the natural grace of an athlete.

By now, they had reached the far end of the park, in a secluded area, surrounded by May trees in full blossom, and with a park bench.

"Shall we sit down for a few minutes?" he asked.

"Yes, that would be nice. It is so beautiful here."

As a gentleman, he waited for her to sit down first and then he sat down himself a little distance from her. Unobtrusively, she moved close to him and close enough so that he was just aware of her perfume. Her subtle movement caused her pretty dress to ride up a little, which gave Lionel a tantalising glimpse of the lovely white lace at the hem of her petticoat. She quickly and modestly readjusted her dress.

Now that he was sitting close to a girl whom he found stunningly attractive, his old shyness came back. He felt the urge to hold her in his arms and kiss her, but his inhibitions stopped that. (He did not sense what her feelings were and that a kiss from him even on a first date might be on her agenda.) He tried to say how he was feeling about her but the words would not come out. There was an embarrassed silence, she looked at him patiently and with affection, sensing that he was trying to tell her something close to his heart.

Then he said rather hesitantly, "Marielle, I really like you very much. I think you are lovely."

It was a very simple sentiment, which could have been expressed better, but his simplicity and sincerity touched her heart. No one had ever said such a nice thing to her and in such a sincere way.

She smiled at him and said very gently, "I like you too. You are very nice and I would like to know you better."

There was then another pause, and she instinctively held his hand in an empathetic and affectionate way.

Finding this comforting and exciting at the same time, he whispered, "I would like you to be my friend."

"Do you mean girlfriend?"

He was choked with emotion and unable to speak, so he just nodded.

Then she decided to tease him a little to ease the tension, "As a high-powered businessman who travels the country, you must have a girlfriend in every town and village and maybe a pretty wife at home waiting for you with open arms."

Having said this, she immediately regretted having done so. He had told her that he did not have a girlfriend and she guessed that this might be a sore point for him.

He realised that her comments were intended to be kind and that she was a very sweet person, but they did indeed touch a raw nerve in him, as he felt inadequate at never having any sort of romantic life, even though many of his mates were married by now. He also longed for female company and affection. Work pressures plus his shyness had got in the way. He felt himself blushing and was impelled to express his deep feelings, speaking without any hint of self-pity, "Ever since I started with the company I have worked flat out. Particularly since I have been on the road. It is a hard graft, the way I do it. Not just the good clients for me. I keep looking for new clients. I get lots of rejections but keep going. Travelling long distances can be tough. Most hotels are not brilliant like yours. By the time I get home, I am often exhausted. No time for social life or girlfriends."

She felt real sympathy for him. He had said a lot about himself in a few words. She then looked at him with her lovely brown eyes and said in a very affectionate tone, "If I were your girlfriend, I might like you to kiss me."

He paused and looked lovingly at her. Then he took her in his arms and they kissed. It was a moment of magic for both of them. Their love affair had begun. He sighed. "Oh, Marielle."

She then put her arms gently around his neck, whispered, "You dear boy." And kissed him tenderly on his lips. She must have found a sweet spot, as a tingle ran all the way down his spine. For a moment, his legs felt like jelly. She was his first girlfriend but he knew he was in love with her. Her feelings for him were just the same, although he did not fully recognise it at the time.

After a while, it dawned on him what was happening to him and he could not really believe it. The lovely Marielle was beautiful, had dark hair and brown eyes, with a Mediterranean appearance. She was elegant, smartly dressed and graceful. Everything that Aunt Rose had predicted. He did not mention this to Marielle but he felt even more convinced that his feelings of love for her were absolutely genuine and were his destiny.

As they had time to spare, they walked on into the nearby pinewoods and kissed and held each other some more. She could feel how strong his arms were and thought, *If he kept hold of me, I might not be able to escape.* She also thought that she might not want to escape.

Marielle could also tell from the way he looked at her that there was true love in his eyes. His tender kisses told the same story; he did not need words to express his feelings for her.

As they were getting ready to leave the park, he said that he was coming back to the area in two weeks' time, having done such good business this time. Whilst holding her hand in his, he said very slowly and deliberately, "Marielle, I am in love with you."

With a tear in her eye, she responded very quietly and sincerely, "Lionel, we hardly know each other. You have not had a girlfriend and may never have kissed a girl. I am sure you are sincere and I like you very much. I would love to see you again in two weeks' time. If you still think you are in love with me then, maybe I won't doubt you again."

She longed to tell him that she loved him but felt that this was a first date. Let things settle. She also noticed how he was looking more intently at her now, particularly her hair and her eyes. It was as if something in him had happened. She knew he really was in love with her.

He spoke again, "I really want to see you again and for us to write to each other."

"I would love to spend time with you again and perhaps we might go out somewhere for a day. I will send you a love letter in a pink envelope, with a hint of perfume on it, so that your family will know that you have a girlfriend."

"I will write to you every day. I will also let you know the exact day when I am coming back here. It would be wonderful to spend a whole day together."

Chapter Nine

They left the park, hand in hand, and had to go their separate ways. Lionel started his journey back to Lyon, and Marielle caught her bus and met her sister, Véronique, "Véro", for lunch at a café in St Auban, where she worked as a nurse at the main hospital. Véro on seeing Marielle said, "You have a sparkle in your eye today, little Sis. Has something happened?"

"Yes, Véro, I have met a really lovely man, and he is going to come and see me on his next visit to this area.

"He's good-looking with fair hair and blue eyes. Smartly dressed and has good manners. His name is Lionel. He has a smart Citroën and is a sales representative for a firm in Lyon. I met him when I was working in the reference library and he was collecting information about the area. He has been staying at the hotel. He is single and lives with his mum and grandma. He is a bit shy, that's probably why he is still single."

Véro looked sceptical.

"Take care, young lady. Commercial travellers! That all sounds great, but don't commercial travellers have a bit of a reputation? And how about a shy salesman? Doesn't ring true to me. But then I am a sceptical nurse."

Marielle replied, "I am sure that he is absolutely genuine. He will be coming back here in two weeks' time, and we will go out together. If possible, I might have time to introduce him to you."

Véro responded, "Let's hope he turns out better than your previous boyfriends. I don't want to see you get hurt, sweetie."

"He's completely different. Much more grown-up, polite and hard-working. They both dumped me because I was not willing to go to bed with them. I am no longer at all religious, but I was brought up a catholic and don't like the idea of sex outside marriage."

"What would you do if this Lionel guy wants to take you to bed?"

Marielle was taken aback by this direct question and she paused and replied very thoughtfully, "When I know him better, I might know the answer to that."

When they had finished their meals, Véro said, "I have always been in favour of sex before marriage, as and when I find a chap that I really like, which has happened sometimes. Apart from being enjoyable, it gives experience, which can help whether you get married or not. Sex after marriage can be routine and boring."

Marielle responded. "Surely, Mum and Dad still love each other and have a good sex life, even at their ages."

Véro laughed and said, "They are not that old even now. Mum was only nineteen when they got married. I have never spied on them after bedtime, but I guess Steph may have tried to do so."

Marielle smiled at that thought. She wondered how her relationship with Lionel might work out. Things had happened so very quickly.

Before they parted, Véro said, "I really love your dress, it's gorgeous."

"It's one I made from Mum's old 1940s' pattern book. I love the style and the lower skirt length."

Véro responded, "When not at work, I normally wear a mini-skirt these days. I am not pretty like you, but I have good legs and like to show them off as my best feature."

Marielle replied, "You have a lovely face."

The sisters embraced fondly and then went their separate ways.

Chapter Ten

On his homeward journey, Lionel stopped off for the night with his good friend, André and his wife, Nicole at Dijon, where André was an agent for the company. Lionel had known Nicole from the tennis club at Lyon, where they had sometimes been doubles partners. He told them how good the business trip had been, with so many orders. He said that many of the retailers had really old-fashioned goods far inferior to those of the company. He intended to visit again and also to try his luck in Belgium.

He could not avoid mentioning Marielle: indeed he spoke about her at length. Nicole said that she sounded wonderful and worthy of a fine man like Lionel, who responded that he was very surprised that she liked him so much.

"I am not good-looking or anything or very clever. I am just a boring salesman from Lyon, who has never managed to find a girlfriend."

André responded, "You are a brilliant salesman and a very likeable chap. You are always polite and courteous and win over customers with your enthusiasm and deep knowledge of the products."

Nicole interrupted, "Who told you that you were not good-looking? You are well built and strong, with fair curly hair and blue eyes. Just the sort of thing that can appeal to a girl.

"You dress smartly and carry yourself well. Some ladies at the tennis club fancied you."

"I thought they were just fooling and trying to embarrass me."

"The way that they looked at you told me otherwise. And what about your fast first service. That would surely impress the ladies and your new girl."

"Maybe not. She was a regional level player when a junior and is still I expect a good club-level player."

"I think your Marielle is a lucky girl. If she has you on the hook, she would be wise to reel you in, as you are a really nice guy who would make her a good husband."

André asked whether the hotel was okay.

Lionel replied, enthusiastically, "It was excellent in all ways, the food, the service, the comfort. Not too expensive. I had a strange feeling at times, however, about the village, particularly the old converted building opposite the hotel, as if something strange might have happened in the past. Maybe something took place in one of the world wars. I felt I must have been there before but I know I haven't."

Nicole said the sometimes she had felt that sort of thing about a place.

Before he left, André mentioned to him that there was a rumour that a major retailer in the area and the main customer of the company in that region was having to obtain an urgent loan from the bank. Lionel, conscientious as ever, took note of this useful local information.

He left Dijon the next day and on his journey could not stop thinking of Marielle.

Was it all a dream? Would she still feel the same about him when he returned? Would she really write him a love letter in a pink envelope?

He thought that she was the girl of his dreams and then corrected himself. He could not have dreamt of or imagined someone as wonderful as Marielle. She was, however, the girl that Aunt Rose had predicted, down to the last detail.

When Lionel got back to Lyon, Martha, his mother, could not fail to see that he was in a very happy mood. He told her and Esther about Marielle, and they were pleased that at last he was showing interest in the opposite sex. This dispelled the fears that he might be a homo. Martha also felt that at twenty-eight, it was about time he thought about getting settled with the right young lady and getting a place of his own. Esther was very amused when a pink love letter landed on the door mat, while Lionel was out at work. In the evening, he read the letter to himself and later rather naïvely read it aloud to his mother and his grandmother.

"My darling Lionel,

I am missing you so much already and cannot wait for you to come back. That time we spent together in the park was the happiest time of my life. I keep thinking about you and want to hold you in my arms. I hope we can find time for a day out together. I have several ideas for places to go, depending on the weather. I do hope our relationship will continue and grow stronger.

With all my love,

Marielle"

His mother was surprised by the tone of the letter, which was quite explicit and unequivocal. She was also pleased for him, and added, "That was some love letter!"

He also wrote love letters to Marielle and returned to Moulins several times during the year, as it was a good area for doing business, and also, of course, to spend time with his lovely girlfriend. Their relationship got ever closer and became really serious. But were there to be storm clouds, as predicted by the fortune-teller?

Chapter Eleven

On his second visit to Moulins, he and Marielle managed to spend a whole day together, despite their work commitments. They left the hotel in his car after breakfast, going along the old road towards the end of the bypass and the main route towards Belgium. Before leaving the old road, Lionel pulled up in a layby, and Marielle wondered why, but not for long.

"Marielle I love you so much, and I am so happy to be with you."

He then took her in his arms and kissed her tenderly.

"I know you are in love with me, dear Lionel, and, if you didn't already know, I am madly in love with you."

They continued their journey on what proved to be a wonderful and meaningful day. They spent it at Martinsville Lake over the border in Belgium. This was a large man-made lake in a woodland setting with a few small timber lakeside bars, cafés and other low-key leisure facilities. Their day began with coffee in a lakeside bar, and a discussion as to what to do.

They saw that there were timber rowing boats for hire and decided to hire one and row to the far side of the lake, where there was a nature trail. They both liked the boat: the timber was well-varnished and it had a solid feel to it. Lionel asked

Marielle whether she could swim, and to his surprise, she said that once a week she swam two kilometres in the local swimming pool. She pointed out that, if they fell in, the problem would be the low water temperature. Lionel confirmed that he was a strong swimmer, but fully understood what she had said about the water temperature.

She then suggested that she should row the boat on the outward trip and that he should do so on the return trip. He was surprised that she wanted to row but was happy to agree. The boatman, who was not the most cheerful person, explained that there were two lifebelts in the boat and also a siren if they should get into difficulties. He advised them to return if the wind got up or if the mist moved in. It was cloudy but warm and dry.

"It looks alright now but the weather can change here in an instant and the lake can become dangerous. I had to rescue a couple like you only last week."

With due warning of the risks of rowing on a lake, they set off with Marielle on the oars and Lionel in the stern with the rudder. He was amazed at how beautifully she rowed the boat, smoothly, rhythmically and without great effort. Although slim, she was clearly fit and athletic, with good muscle tone. The boat made good progress and maintained a very straight course. Confident at what she was doing, she was obviously enjoying the exercise and was glowing with health and fitness. The gentle breezes had disturbed her neat hairstyle, but this made her seem even more attractive to him.

He came to see her as much more than just a charming girl, who looked great in a nice dress. She was also an outdoor girl, graceful and talented with whom he could enjoy outdoor activities. They reached the far side of the lake; she was far from fatigued as she expertly tied the boat up at the quay, and they disembarked.

"You are excellent at rowing," he said.

"Thank you, kind sir."

"You looked so pretty when you were rowing."

"Thank you again, kind sir."

He loved being teased by her and responded, "That sort of talk gets young ladies kissed."

"That wouldn't be too bad," was her cheeky response.

He took her in his arms and gave her a tender kiss. She smiled and laid her head on his shoulder.

"How did you learn to row so well?"

"Dad taught the three of us how to swim and then how to row. We often went to lakes or rivers for days out. Véro and I listened to Dad and learnt quickly. Steph found it boring and often, with her on the oars, the boat just went around in circles. She saw no point in rowing when you could have a motorboat."

Hand in hand and feeling very happy, they took a short walk into the woods, where they did some bird-watching, and then headed back to the quay where they embarked, with Lionel taking the oars and Marielle at the stern. The sun had broken through the clouds and the weather was fair, with little wind. Lionel rowed powerfully but with little finesse, and the boat moved slower than with Marielle on the oars. Nevertheless, she felt confident with him, although there tended to be a drift to port. With the summer sun, the lake changed its appearance. Instead of just all dark green, it was now a patchwork of different shades of green, with areas of bright reflection from the full sunlight. It was like an impressionist painting, with dreamy pine woods in the background.

A surreal image came into her mind of a whole life in a boat with Lionel on the oars. She felt that whether the waters were calm or stormy, they would be safe, as he would be steadfast, loyal and strong. The thought left her but may have etched itself somewhere in her subconscious.

They reached the shore and handed the boat over to the boatman, who commented, "You were lucky with the weather. Fortunately, I did not need to rescue you like that young couple last week."

They had lunch at a nearby café, which they much enjoyed after the fresh air and exercise. The weather was now very warm and pleasant. Lionel brought out a rug from his car, and they found a quiet grassy place to lie down together on the rug. Lionel was lying on his back and occasionally Marielle would lean over him and kiss him on his neck.

Lying next to her, he began to feel a very strong sexual attraction to her, which made him feel embarrassed. His hormones were going wild. It did not help that Marielle kept leaning over him with a loving smile and gently kissing him. He was reluctant to say anything but was looking troubled, which she began to notice.

"What's the matter, sweetie? Are you not comfortable?"

He knew he needed to say something, but struggled to find the words. She gave him her affectionate smile and remembered how he had found it hard to say what he had wanted to on the park bench at Moulins.

"Marielle," he whispered, "I am finding you very attractive and feel a strong urge to make love to you. I am sorry, but I need to tell you. I have not been in a relationship before and everything is new to me. Dare I ask you whether you are expecting us to make love?"

She replied in a serious tone, "Most young people in relationships these days think it is okay and even normal to make love, but I am not the same. I am not really religious anymore but was brought up as a Catholic, and still believe that love-making is very precious and is for married couples."

Then she could not hold back a tear.

"I have had two boyfriends. Paul was an old school friend but he dropped me when I refused to go to bed with him. I was only eighteen at the time.

"Roger was a friend from the tennis club and he was just the same. When I refused, he was also horrible and said that I was frigid. I would be broken-hearted if I was to lose you, as I know that I am in love with you. We are both now older and people of our age do make love if not married."

Lionel sat up and took her tenderly in his arms.

"Darling Marielle, I would never do anything to hurt you. I would not want to make love to you unless you wholeheartedly wanted me to do so and not just to keep me. I was also brought up through the synagogue to believe that marriage was sacred and that sex was for married couples. It may be hard, but I will be your boyfriend and friend but no more unless at some stage we both decide otherwise. I never want to do anything to hurt you."

She cried but they were the tears of love and happiness at being with such a truly good man and friend. She remembered that, when they had been together on the park bench in Moulins, she had said that she wanted to get to know him better. Now she was feeling that she had done so and that he was a very genuine and sincere person. He had been so frank with her about this serious matter, where he had strong feelings.

She said, "Thank you for being so open with me. We must always try to share things like that."

She had a sad thought that she would soon need to share something with him but now was not the right moment. After taking tea at a café, they made their way back to Moulins, and later that week, he had to return to Lyon. They both felt that after this visit, they had become much closer to each other.

On his next visit, work pressures prevailed, as he had to travel as far as the north coast, as part of his business trip. He did manage to spend two very happy hours alone with Marielle.

He had a longer visit to Moulins in September but was still very busy with work. Although there was not enough time for a day out together, Marielle arranged for them to play tennis at her club in St Auban, in the late afternoon.

They changed at the club and emerged in their tennis clothes, she in a smart white tennis dress which showed off her figure and her shapely legs and he in shorts and a tennis shirt, showing his strong arms and legs. She imagined that he could hit a tennis ball very hard. She had arranged for them to play a set of mixed doubles with friends of hers from the club, who were good players.

Before they met the other couple, there was time for her to check out his fast first serve. She took him to a spare court and stood at the side of the court, whilst he served several times in each court. His serve was very fast and accurate. Then she asked him to serve to her as fast as he liked, but he was reluctant to do so.

"I am afraid that I might hit you."

"Don't worry. I am an experienced player with fast reactions. I can get out of the way even if you serve body-line."

On his first serve to her, she got the ball on to her racket, but retuned it into the net, just failing to clear the net. He served twice more to the same court and each time, she returned the ball at speed just short of the base-line on his side. The same happened when she was on the other court, except once when she hit the return into the net. She returned the other services to his base-line, at speed, some on her backhand and some on her forehand. He was amazed at her skill and told her how impressed he was.

She then spoke to him about his service, which she said was excellent, and which would trouble most club players, men or women. She said, however, that she could judge from the way he tossed the ball and from his service action where the ball was likely to go. A good coach could help him disguise the line the ball would take and wrong-foot his opponent. She also pointed out that his serve was straight up and down with no deviation from spin: again, coaching could teach him to use spin.

Some men might have felt daunted to receive such advice from a young woman, but not Lionel. One of his great virtues was that, although he was very competitive and keen to succeed, he was never resentful of someone who performed better at something than he did. He was always willing to learn from others who were more skilled or knowledgeable than he was and to try to do better. He was happy to take advice from a woman, perhaps because women had been so important in his upbringing, his mother and grandmother both being intelligent and practical people. Later, as a manager, his ability to listen to others, including his staff, was one of the reasons for his success.

They played the tennis set and won a closely fought match, partly through Lionel's serves and partly because of Marielle's excellent returns.

That evening, they went to Véro's apartment, where she served them supper. She had to leave at 8.30 to go on her night shift. As she left, she said mischievously, "I will leave you lovebirds now. Have fun! There is a nice double-bed in my spare room. It's very bouncy. In the bedside drawer, there is a selection of condoms, both for protection and for an enhanced experience."

They did not take up the offer but had a very happy hour in each other's company, expressing their deep love. They were, however, quite impressed with Vero's professionalism in the sphere of sexual activity.

Lionel was not able to return until November, as he had to visit Marseille, where a rival firm had moved in, importing goods from Italy and Germany. He had to ensure that his clients were happy with the service he was providing and would not wish to change over to the new company. He also had to go to Burgundy, where the major customer at Dijon had gone into liquidation. He was able to find some new outlets there, which went down very well with his boss in Lyon. He and Marielle continued writing to each other and made a few phone calls, more difficult and costly in those days.

Eventually, he managed to return to Moulins in November and spent some time with Marielle. She could not express to him just how much she had missed him and he felt just the same. He noticed that she was a little sad and wondered if anything was the matter. On the afternoon of the 18th November, they went into the park at Moulins, retracing their steps from the previous spring. They kissed under the old oak tree, and he said to her that he could not live without her. The weather was mild for November and the autumn sun brought a mellow warmth to the day, reminding them of their wonderful time there in May.

As he talked of the possibility of marriage, Marielle became strangely quiet and said, "I have something difficult to tell you, darling. There is a problem with my dad. He keeps telling me to break off our relationship."

With anxiety and sadness, she explained the family history of anti-Semitism.

"He actually seems to respect you personally but cannot at the moment accept the idea of me marrying a Jewish man."

Lionel was surprised more than shocked, as he had never experienced any anti-Semitism in his life, not since he was bullied in school. He thought that in secular France, anti-Semitism was dead. He looked very despondent. *Was he going to lose the girl he loved because he was Jewish?*

Marielle took him in her arms. She assured him that she would persuade her dad not to oppose their getting married. She said, "Just give me a little time. I know I can persuade him to change his mind."

Lionel felt somewhat reassured. He also thought of Aunt Rose, and of the difficulties to be expected in the love affair, which would be overcome.

Marielle said that she would not be at the hotel that evening, as she and Véro were going to visit an elderly relative in hospital. She would, however, see him at breakfast the next morning.

Chapter Twelve

That evening, 18th November 1968, Lionel went back to the hotel, delighted with the orders he had achieved for the company's products, but a little anxious about the future of his relationship with Marielle. He was left with a feeling that things might go wrong, but there was still Aunt Rose's prediction of difficulties, which would be overcome. Perhaps Gaston Leclerc was that difficulty.

He decided, however, that in view of his business success, he deserved a really good evening meal and selected dishes from the à la carte menu. The meal was really excellent. Fish Soup, Roast Guinea Fowl followed by a superb chocolate gateau. He did not normally drink any alcohol, but on this occasion, he allowed himself a glass of fine cognac at the end of the meal. The drink went down so well that he had a second one.

At eleven o'clock, he retired to his bedroom, where, as was his usual custom, he read his newspaper. The main story was of a serious train crash at Toulon, with many fatalities. There had been a visit to the site by the President. Being tired, Lionel went to bed and fell into a light sleep.

At midnight, something quite extraordinary happened. He heard the strident sound of the whistle of a steam train followed by the hissing of the locomotive and then the drumming of the carriage wheels on the rails. Then the train was gone into the distance. Lionel sat up in bed rubbing his eyes.

There's no railway at Moulins, he thought. *Was I lost in a dream or something?*

The experience was so vivid that he found himself shaking and perspiring. He kept looking out of the bedroom window, but there was nothing to see. He slept very little that night.

In the morning, Marielle was there, looking as lovely as ever, and served him breakfast.

"My love," she said, "you look worried. Have you seen a ghost?"

"Tell me," he asked, "is there a railway in the village?"

"No, the nearest one is well over 10 kilometres to the north, the main line to Paris."

"At midnight, I felt convinced I heard a steam train very near the hotel. Maybe a nightmare after the cognac I had last night and the news of the accident at Toulon."

"Perhaps, but it is most strange." These were her anxious words as she returned to the kitchen. It was rare for Marielle to look so worried.

He also wondered whether what Marielle had told him the previous day about her dad's views had affected his sleep and his state of mind.

Then another customer approached Lionel and said very politely, "Excuse me, sir, but I overheard your conversation with the waitress. I would strongly advise you to speak to Amédée at the tabac. He is very intelligent and knows all about the history of this area."

"Thank you, sir. I think I will do that."

After breakfast, Lionel crossed the road to get to the tabac. A non-smoker, he bought some sweets for the return journey to Lyon and then asked the lady at the counter if he might speak to Amédée.

"Why?" she asked, looking rather anxious. "He is elderly and in poor health."

"It's about a steam train."

The lady became pale and was trembling. "Wait a moment, please."

A few moments later, Amédée appeared. Tall and thin, he had the look of a wizard. Lionel told him what had happened in the night, in graphic detail.

"Sir, you have heard the Ghost Train," Amédée affirmed. "During the Great War, a railway ran through the village. On 18th November 1918, there was a terrible accident. A passenger train from Belgium, bringing home soldiers after the Armistice, was in collision with a goods train, carrying petrol. A huge fire broke out and about one hundred soldiers were killed. It was not possible to identify the bodies of some thirty of them, but some items belonging to passengers were retrieved from the wreckage, cigarette cases, pipes, and penknives…They are still kept at the Town Hall museum. If someone hears the Ghost Train on an anniversary of the accident, it means that his father or grandfather perished in the awful accident."

Lionel was stunned.

"That's impossible," he protested. "My father was shot dead by the Nazis in 1943. My grandfather was killed in Belgium in October 1918. My other grandfather died in Zurich in 1935."

Amédée looked irritated and raising his deep voice proclaimed, "Your father or grandfather died in that accident. The Ghost Train never lies...never!"

Then Amédée left and the lady, who had overheard the conversation, came back behind the counter looking even more worried. Lionel was utterly shocked by this strange episode.

Back home in Lyon, Lionel told the story to Martha and Esther.

"It was just a nightmare," he concluded. "That Amédée chap is crazy."

Then Esther became uncharacteristically agitated. She went into her bedroom where she opened a drawer, took out an old letter, and coming back into the lounge where the others were, quietly read out some extracts.

"Ministry of War 25th October 1918...your husband, Jacob Isaac Steinfeld, is reported missing in action, after a sudden surprise attack by the enemy..."

Martha then interjected, "Jacob could have survived the attack and travelled on that train. He surely would have had personal possessions on him."

Esther, still shaken, left the room and returned carrying two photographs of Jacob proudly holding an impressive pocket watch in his hand. The second photo showed the back of the watch and on the casing, you could clearly see a Star of David and his initials engraved. Esther was in tears. Lionel thought it was the first time he had ever seen her cry. She said that his father had given it to him at his Bar Mitzvah, and it was always his most prized possession. The photos were taken later on and shortly before the outbreak of war.

The family had a very emotional discussion and knew that they had to follow up on this matter, however crazy Amédée might have been. School term would end the next week, so Martha would be able to go to Moulins with Lionel, who was able to arrange a business trip there.

So in December 1968, Lionel and Martha made the long journey to Moulins. Martha was impressed with the company Citroën and with her son's excellent driving.

At Moulins, they checked into the hotel and spent the night there. Martha shared her son's enthusiasm for the hotel. Martha was disappointed that Marielle was not there that evening, as she was very keen to meet her.

The next morning, they found the museum and arranged to see the curator, who had charge of the items rescued from that train. Martha showed the photographs to the curator at the museum, who after a careful search produced the watch shown in the photographs. It was damaged and charred, but you could still clearly see the engravings. Martha and Lionel were stunned. They could not believe what had happened. They packed up the watch carefully, along with the photographs, and thanked the curator very sincerely. She was equally moved, particularly to have a deceased person identified after such a long time and in the fiftieth anniversary year of the Great War.

A few days later, they travelled back to Lyon to tell Esther what they had discovered. When Martha gave the watch to Esther back at their apartment, Esther sobbed and held it to her heart.

"My dear Jacob died with his comrades on that train."

Sadly, Esther passed away after Christmas and was buried with the watch held in her hand. It was as if the news of how

Jacob had died had made her want to join him in the next world. Many attended her funeral not just from the synagogue but also from the wider community, as she was so well-known and well-liked in the city. Among the many letters and cards of condolence, there was one from Marielle, which was much appreciated by Martha. She felt it was sad that Esther had never met Marielle, or would never see her grandson happily married.

If we go forward to the autumn of 1969, Martha and Lionel decided to carry out a light-hearted experiment by staying in the Hotel du Centre on the night of 18th November, the anniversary of the fateful train crash. Martha was allowed special leave from the lycée. The principal was fascinated by the whole story of the train crash and the ghost train with its message from the past. Lionel was able to combine the visit with a business trip.

At midnight, they listened attentively, but no train was heard, only the church clock striking midnight and the hooting of the owls in the park. Lionel turned to his mother, "That proves that ghosts don't exist."

Martha replied in the words of Hamlet to Horatio, "There are more things in heaven and earth, Lionel, than are dreamt of in your philosophy."

Lionel, whilst not saying anything, was inclined to agree with his mother and with Prince Hamlet, particularly when he thought of Aunt Rose and her prediction of his future.

Chapter Thirteen

Lionel could never altogether let himself believe that he had heard a ghost train or even that such things existed. But the accuracy of Aunt Rose's prediction of his future was always in the back of his mind.

He wondered whether Amédée was indeed mad or was some sort of wizard. On his visit with his mother to Moulins in December 1968, Marielle had advised him to go and see Antoinette, the niece of Amédée, who was the co-owner with him of the tabac, and who could tell him all about Amédée's life and background. Marielle said that the old gentleman always had a sleep in the afternoon and that Antoinette could speak to Lionel, at that time of day, without her uncle being present.

Antoinette was a friendly and gentle person: always neatly dressed and very precise and accurate in her work and in dealings with others. These qualities no doubt helped make her successful in her business.

And so Lionel and Antoinette met in the tabac one afternoon in December 1968 and sipped coffee while she told him about her uncle's life. It was obvious that she was devoted to and very fond of her uncle.

"I will begin with the Battle of the Marne, which you may know took place in September 1914, and in which Amédée fought in the French army. He was born in Moulins and was only twenty-one at the time of this battle. Wars are often fought by the very young, with their whole life before them, and often sadly caused by the stupidity of the older generation."

Lionel nodded his assent to these sentiments.

"This battle raged between the Germans, who had invaded France and were aiming to capture Paris, and on the other side, the French army and their allies. In the end, the Germans were driven back and withdrew towards Flanders.

"Amédée suffered a serious wound in his thigh and was taken on a stretcher to a military hospital where he remained for three months. Happily, he recovered but afterwards he needed to walk with a stick. He was discharged from further military service, and, after a year, he obtained employment as a history teacher in a prestigious lycée in Paris, where he remained throughout the war.

"He was a brilliant man and loved teaching, and sharing his knowledge and understanding with the young. His lessons went well and the pupils did well in exams.

"On 18th November 1918, his life was changed for ever. That date was ever etched in his mind.

"His father, Jean Fontaine, was the Stationmaster at Moulins, where the family home was situated. His wife had been struck down with the Spanish flu and was in hospital in St Auban seriously ill. Jean had just been to visit her. Having arrived late back at the station, exhausted and worried, he made a catastrophic error. He permitted a passenger train for Paris to depart before the arrival of a freight train transporting motor fuel and heading for Belgium. On the single line to the west of Moulins, the two trains crashed head-on. It was a horrific accident, with many fatalities, especially French soldiers returning home after the war. Three days later, Jean's wife died in the hospital and he was totally shattered. The shame, the guilt and the grief drove him to suicide. He took his own life in the station building; he was found by a porter hanging from a roof beam.

"This was a catastrophe for Amédée, such an intelligent and sensitive person, to lose his father and his mother in such tragic circumstances. After that, he devoted his life to his profession of teaching and historical research. As he admits himself, he has always been an introvert. He spent years trying to suppress his memories of those dreadful days. He never married or had any close friends.

"I had the tabac in Paris near the lycée where he worked. He had been so helpful and supportive of me, when my mother was terminally ill with cancer. I could not have managed without him at that terrible time.

"He carried on with his career as a teacher and he also became a distinguished historian, writing several history textbooks, from the period of Clovis and the Franks right up to the Franco-Prussian War of 1871–2. With his salary plus the royalties from his books, he was quite well off financially.

"During the Second World War, he continued his career as a history teacher in Paris but became depressed particularly when German soldiers were marching in the Champs Elysée. At the end of the war in 1945, he suffered a nervous breakdown, no longer being able to suppress his memories of the terrible events at Moulins in 1918. He spent some months in a mental hospital, where fortunately he slowly and gradually got better. When he left there, he moved in with me and I looked after him, which I have continued to do ever since. It is a labour of love, as he is always so kind and appreciative. He had to retire from teaching, after the breakdown. I have never married, and looking after my uncle gave a real purpose to my life. He continued studying and writing about history, both national and local. I wish I could have helped him in this but I did not have the brains.

"Towards the end of 1945, we became business partners. I sold my tabac business in Paris and we pooled our resources and purchased the old station building at Moulins. The railway had closed in the 1930s and the building had been occupied by the Germans during the war. This was the building where his father had died by his own hand in 1918. Amédée had decided to confront his demons in a very direct way. We renovated the building, which was in a dreadful state and converted it into three units, a shop, a tabac and a traditional café-bar. We retained and ran the tabac and let the other two units.

"He loved talking to people about current affairs, politics, history and many other subjects.

"In the evening after dinner, he often spent an hour or so in the Café-Bar, sipping a beer and chatting to the other customers in his usual easy manner. They seemed to like him, although he might have seemed a little strange to them. They appreciated in particular his vast knowledge of history, including the local history of this area.

"One evening, an old fellow claimed that he had heard a steam train passing through the village on the night of 18th November in the previous year. He said that his father had died in the accident in 1918. Amédée thought he was a yokel who had drunk too much eau de vie. This is an area of heavy drinking. Fortunately, Amédée drank modestly and avoided spirits. But from time to time other customers told exactly the same story. Always the night of 18th November, the midnight train, the death of a father or grandfather in the accident of 1918. After some years, Amédée became convinced that the stories were true, and spoke to me about them. I did not believe in ghosts or ghost trains and became worried that he might be heading for another nervous breakdown. I suggested to him that the locals in the bar enjoyed fantasising and romanticising. I was concerned about keeping his mental health stable.

"When last month, you, M. Steinfeld, a young business man, intelligent, well-dressed and from another part of France came to the tabac and spoke of the steam train, I became very anxious, as you may have noticed, but my uncle was convinced that your father or grandfather had died in the accident. When he later learnt that your grandfather had indeed died in that way, he believed the truth of the stories without any shadow of doubt and still does to this day."

Lionel was visibly moved by her account of Amédée's eventful and challenging life, and he thanked her most sincerely for telling him Amédée's story.

As he was preparing to leave, he said to her, "Like you, I don't believe in ghosts or the supernatural, but I can understand how your uncle would do so. All the same, I was amazed to discover that my grandfather had died in the train crash. The sounds I heard or thought I heard on that night were incredibly vivid."

While expressing these thoughts, he brought to mind Aunt Rose and her amazing predictions.

In March 1969, Amédée Fontaine died a contented man and at peace with himself. You might say that the steam train had blown away his demons.

His funeral took place at Moulins Church and was attended by over two hundred people, both from the local community and from the academic world. He was a distinguished historian and two professors of history as well as one member of the Académie Française attended to pay their respects. Antoinette and close relatives were the main mourners.

Antoinette grieved for him then and for the rest of her life, but took comfort from the fact that he had passed away at peace and free from mental anguish, which had so troubled him in his earlier years. She took comfort in the size of the attendance for the funeral, particularly the academics there, to reflect his distinguished work as a historian.

Chapter Fourteen

During the visit to Moulins in December 1968, when Lionel and his mother, Martha, were staying at the hotel in connection with their visit to the museum, Lionel introduced Marielle to his mother. He feared they might not get on, but it was obvious that they really liked each other. They found it easy to talk about a range of things, including fashion, cuisine, their family histories, and the places where they lived. Martha found Marielle quite adorable, so charming and natural, easy to talk to and genuinely interested in what Martha had to say.

That evening, Martha said to Lionel, "That girl is delightful. It is obvious from the way she looks at you that she is in love with you. You should surely ask her to marry you. What are you waiting for?"

Then Lionel had to explain to Martha the problem with Marielle's father, and in doing so mentioned the Dreyfus Affair. Martha was not shocked. She said, "Anti-Semitism never goes away. It can rear its ugly head anywhere. I am surprised that anyone still thinks that Dreyfus was guilty."

She continued, "Perhaps Marielle will have to choose between her father and you, poor girl."

Lionel never really understood why the Jews were hated in some quarters and asked his mother about it. Over the years they had never talked about anti-Semitism. Lionel thought that with the defeat of Hitler, it was a thing of the past. For Martha, it was a very painful subject and associated with the death of her husband.

As they sat together in the hotel, Martha decided that Lionel needed a lesson in history. She explained,

"The Jews had been persecuted since the time of Christ because the Romans had blamed the Jews for the execution of Jesus. In fact, it was the pro-Roman Jewish leaders in cahoots with the Roman governor of Judea who wanted Jesus killed, as Jesus was opposed to the corruption of the regime in Judea. The spiritual side of Christ's message was lost on the regime. The genuine Jews believed in the one God, and could not accept the polytheism of the Romans. Later, these Jews were willing to fight and die for their beliefs.

"And so things got worse for the Jews when there was a major Jewish revolt against the Romans, which eventually was savagely crushed by the Emperor Titus in 70 AD. The Jews were portrayed as the enemies of Rome, and Titus was seen as a great hero, cementing his position as the second Emperor of the Flavian dynasty. There was a further Jewish revolt at the time of the Emperor Hadrian. The Romans again suppressed it and totally destroyed Jerusalem in 135 AD. This was the final diaspora of the Jewish people, who fled to other lands, to be persecuted as enemies of Rome and also of Christianity, which under the Emperors Constantine and later Theodosius became the religion of the Roman Empire.

"The Jews as a persecuted minority had to work harder and try harder than others. They excelled in many fields, including finance and banking, scholarship, science and music. This has led to a degree of envy, particularly by the

Nazis, who blamed the Jews for the decline of Germany between the two wars. You and I have both worked exceptionally hard to do well in our careers and maybe that is something which came from our Jewish heritage. I don't know.

"In more recent times, the creation of the modern State of Israel has caused serious political division and unrest. Two peoples, the Israelis and the Palestinians, each believe that they have the sole right to occupy the same territory. Jews generally are now sometimes blamed for actions of the Israel government."

Martha ended by saying, "Anti-Semitism is now rare, particularly after the holocaust, but it stills crops up."

Lionel responded by thanking his mother, but he added, "I know that I am Jewish, and I am certainly not ashamed of my heritage, but my main feeling is that I am French and a citizen of the Republic, where one can practice any religion or none. I do not know whether being Jewish has made me work harder, or whether it was because we were poor when I grew up. I think it was the latter."

Martha reacted by saying, "We were poor because we were Jewish. If your father had not been Jewish, he would not have ended up in a German concentration camp. It is sometimes hard to explain what causes what. I too feel French and my race and religion have never changed that. I am proud of your feelings for the French Republic, which I hope will always be a force for good in the world."

Chapter Fifteen

In spite of constant efforts, Marielle was not able to persuade her father to change his mind. He kept repeating, "You are too young to settle down. You need to meet other lads and visit other countries. You are only twenty-two. There is plenty of time before you need to think of marriage."

Gaston did not mention that Sandrine was only nineteen when he married her.

He never mentioned that Lionel was Jewish but she knew that this was his real reason for opposing their relationship.

She was fighting a losing battle and got more and more depressed, very unlike Marielle.

In January 1969, she talked seriously to her sister, Véro, who had a robust view about love, men, life and everything else.

Firstly, they spoke about anti-Semitism and how they both disapproved of it. Véro said that she really disliked her grandpa and his views.

"He seems to regard the Jews as inhuman aliens. Also the Gipsies and the Algerians. Strangely, he does not seem bothered about black people. Dad says that it was because West Africans fought bravely against the Prussians, some time ago. They must have made a good impression on the

French regiments at the time. The regiment has always seemed too important to Grandpa.

"As a nurse, I tend to all people whatever their race or religion or nationality. They are all human beings who need care and attention at a difficult time in their lives."

Then she spoke to Marielle specifically about Lionel and what to do.

"Your problem, little Sis, is that you always want to please everyone. You were always like that. It's not always possible. Try pleasing yourself for once. You are obviously madly in love with this guy. He is very square and a bit naff, but he is also quite a dishy hulk. With his curly fair hair and blue eyes, he is easy on the eye. Ignore Dad and elope with your bloke. You are over twenty-one and do not need parental consent. After all, it's the swinging sixties, we don't have to obey our parents anymore. Personally, I am not looking to get married. I love my job in nursing, caring for and comforting people who are ill and often frightened. I much prefer this to being married with small children and doing housework all day. I have had several male friends but they know I am not interested in marriage. Not yet anyway."

Marielle hugged her sister but knew that she would be unhappy at eloping and wanted both parents' blessing. Marielle then said, "I am not getting anywhere with Dad. Should I see if Mum would be on my side?"

"It's hard to say as they have always stuck together like glue. Steph and I spent our youth trying to play one off against the other, but never got anywhere, as they always saw through us."

Despite these words of caution, Marielle turned to her mother. She realised that her parents were extremely close to each other and that Sandrine was very loyal to Gaston, whom she loved and admired greatly. She was of a generation in which some women believed that they should obey their husbands in all things. She and Gaston were also business partners and were seen as always agreeing about everything.

Marielle had no idea that her mother strongly disapproved of the anti-Semitic views of her husband's family. When Gaston had ever expressed such views, Sandrine had remained silent. Sandrine, however, also remembered that her mother's family, having moved to France from Spain, had been subject to hostility from some sections of the public, opposed to immigration.

Marielle approached her mother tentatively but burst into tears as she explained her feelings and wishes. Sandrine was distressed, as Marielle had never cried ever since she was a very small child. Sandrine was very much on Marielle's side but knew she would find it stressful to have an argument with Gaston. She said to her daughter that Gaston was a stubborn as a mule and she would have to talk to him. She added she would be happy to have Lionel as a son-in-law. Sandrine was normally calm and quiet, but deep down was a determined person with fire in her heart, particularly if she felt a sense of injustice, as in the present case.

Chapter Sixteen

For her serious discussion with her husband, Sandrine wisely chose an evening when the restaurant was closed and there were few guests in the hotel. She decided to wear one of her favourite dresses, which she sometimes wore on evenings out. It was in a lovely dark red colour, which suited her well and which Gaston liked very much. She also wore matching earrings and a necklace and arranged her hair to look beautiful. She used her excellent skills in her makeup. She looked very young for her age and her beauty was not lost on Gaston.

Véro had assumed that her parents were still enjoying a regular and happy sex life. You might think so as they were both quite young and good-looking and obviously loved each other. But even nurses do not know everything and looks can be deceptive. In early middle age, life can change. Gaston and Sandrine both worked very hard and had done so for years, with rarely a break or a holiday. Their minds were taken up with the problems of the business. What to do about a chef or a waiter who was not up to standard? What about the next tax return? Could they claim for expenditure on new equipment? All these new rules about food hygiene and staff rights coming out of Brussels. Would the new bypass take away the passing trade? And how would bookings be next year with the predicted recession? When Gaston and Sandrine, at last, got to bed, the most either could manage was to read a book or magazine. They normally just crashed out to sleep.

Sandrine and Gaston were sitting in their lounge, and he noticed how she had dressed and, detecting a certain look in her eye, he sensed what was coming. She was not just there alone but had come with the artillery i.e. all her highly skilled feminine allure. He felt vulnerable as sometimes a man can feel when confronted by a woman who was both beautiful and motivated. She addressed him in a calm and serious tone but could not disguise a trace of emotion in her voice. She loved him so deeply: her husband, her business partner, her best friend, and her hero. But she had to say what needed to be said.

"Gaston Leclerc, we have been married for over twenty-five years and have always been very happy together. We have rarely disagreed about anything, but now I feel distressed by your attitude. There is anti-Semitism in your family, which I find obnoxious. Why should this still exist after the defeat of the Nazis? I love your dad dearly. I cannot forget how good your mum and dad were to me when I moved here from Marseille. I was so far from my family but they were a new mum and dad for me. And all the financial help they gave us when we bought this place, then so derelict. Sadly, when your mum died young, he carried on bravely and was a wonderful granddad to our girls, who rarely showed any affection for him, apart from Marielle.

"You and your dad should forget about the Dreyfus Affair. That man was totally innocent and was framed by the army elite to protect a rogue officer in your grandfather's regiment. Yet you have been influenced by your dad who still believes in his heart that Jews are not loyal to France and may all be traitors or spies. He also thinks they are all too rich and influential."

Gaston listened intently. He was not an over-sensitive person nor a student of history, but a man of action, who liked to get things done. He sensed, however, that Sandrine was finding it hard to say these things to him. He sensed that it was hurting her to express these sentiments as much as it was for him to hear them. He began to feel an overwhelming empathy for her and respect for her courage.

She continued, getting more motivated, "That is ridiculous. Take Lionel for example. His dear father was murdered by the Nazis, and his grandfather fought for France in the Great War and received a gallantry medal. Is Lionel not a good French citizen with that background? He loves the French Republic where we can practice any religion or none. Like you, he supports the Gaullist party.

"He and his family were very poor when they moved to Lyon, and they are now comfortably off only through the hard work of Lionel and his mother. He and Marielle are deeply in love with each other, both wonderful young people. There is no doubt that he will love and provide for our dear daughter. Religion is no bar to their marriage, as they are both agnostic, as we are. I really implore you to approve the marriage and make our dear daughter truly happy."

When she had finished, she felt drained and could not judge what her husband was thinking. His mind was in turmoil. He knew he had no answer and could not refute her arguments. Yet he found it very hard to accept the idea that he could have a Jewish son-in-law. The idea that Jewishness was unpleasant had been ingrained in him for so many years by his father and grandfather.

But he looked at Sandrine full of admiration and love for her. She was the most important thing in his life, ever since they had married and also for the future. Not only his loving wife but his excellent business partner and constant supporter. The last thing he wanted was to undermine their relationship, and he knew that there was every danger that he might do so.

Prejudices cling on, but like a soldier, he could recognise defeat. With a sigh of resignation, he said, "You are right. I will give my approval to this marriage. We will be united, but I hate to think what Dad will think about it, after all the things we have said over the years."

Sandrine was relieved and truly grateful for what he had said but felt very emotional. She knew how hard it might be for him to change his mind over Marielle's love affair. She told him that she loved him dearly and later showed her love for him that night, as she changed into a new short pink satin and lace nightdress, with a matching negligee which she had recently purchased at the new stylish boutique in St Auban. She looked stunning and she still knew how to excite him. They made love in bed for the first time in a while and were so happy together. In fact, they managed it again in the small hours, or au petit matin, as they say in France.

The next morning, she said that she would tell Marielle about their conversation. He replied respectfully that he would prefer to do so himself, as she needed to hear it from him. He added that he bitterly regretted not speaking often enough to Marielle over the years.

He met his daughter in the kitchen, as they were preparing breakfast for the few guests in the hotel that night. He asked her to come over to the office with him. He told her that he and her mother had discussed her relationship with Lionel the previous evening and that he had decided to give his whole-hearted blessing to her relationship with Lionel.

Taking her in his arms he said to her,

"Your happiness is very important to me as well as to your mum. I sometimes feel that I have not always shown enough affection to you. It is well known that I always wanted a son, but that was no reason not to value you as you deserve.

"I really appreciate what a good and affectionate person you are. You have always given us so much wonderful help at the hotel. Nothing has been too much trouble for you. You have always been much more helpful than your sisters."

Still holding her in his arms, he embraced her and then gently let her go.

She was very moved by what he had said, and replied, "You have done so much for me. You taught me how to swim really well, to row boats, to play tennis, to sail boats, to tie knots, to ride horses and always to have a positive attitude. You also trained me to be a good waitress. I really love the hotel and enjoy whatever work is needed here. You and Mum have done such a brilliant job.

"I had a much better childhood than many of my school friends, like Sophie Moreau, for example, whose Dad always treated her as a child and called her 'his little princess'. She was always having to wear pink dresses and was rarely allowed out. She found it embarrassing when he hugged her in front of her friends.

"You were always there for me when help was needed, like that time with the tennis coach."

"Yes, I had to deal with him. I never liked those two boys you went out with. I am glad that you gave them the elbow."

"That's not quite what happened. Each of them dumped me because I refused to go to bed with them."

"I didn't know that. If I had known that they were harassing you, I would have knocked their blocks off."

"Lionel is very different. We have had a serious conversation about the future, neither of us like the idea of sex before marriage. This comes from our religious upbringing in the two different faiths. We both want a proper marriage, fully approved by both our families, and we would like them all to be friends."

"I am very proud of you, Marielle, you are a wonderful daughter: no son could have been as wonderful as you."

She wept a little and managed to smile and whispered, "Now it's time to deal with breakfast. We must not keep the guests waiting!"

Chapter Seventeen

Marielle phoned Lionel later that day, in the hope that he would be at home, which he was, to tell him the wonderful news that her dad had given his warm approval to them getting married. To say he was overjoyed would be an understatement. He missed her so much and wanted them to be together all the time, and she felt exactly the same. Now, at last, they could plan for the wedding.

Marielle, Lionel and Sandrine met at the hotel in the following week to discuss the wedding arrangements. Moulins Church was booked for 31st May, and it was decided that the reception would be at the hotel, which would be closed to guests, but available for wedding guests to stay overnight or longer if necessary. The new head chef, Martine, (who had ambitions for a Michelin Star), would provide the food and the head waiter, Marco, would take charge of the front of house.

Moulins Church was once part of a Cistercian Abbey, founded in the twelfth century. Most of the Abbey was destroyed either in the wake of the French Revolution, or in the world wars, but the Church survived and was consecrated in 1850 as the parish church for the village. Built in the Romanesque style and subsequently altered and partly rebuilt, it retained the impressive character of the Romanesque style: massive structure, thick walls, rounded arches, small windows and fine sculptures and depictions of Biblical scenes.

In the nineteenth century, it was provided with a superb organ, as a result of a donation from a wealthy industrialist. This was a Cavaillé-Coll organ, ranked as one of the five best of that make in northern France. The organ was refurbished in the 1950s, with new electric bellows and electric manuals, in place of the old tracker action. It boasted five manuals, including some superb solo stops.

Many famous organists had given recitals on this prestigious and powerful organ, including César Frank, Camille Saint-Saëns, Louis Vierne, and Charles-Marie Widor. The current organist was Dominique Sarlat, who was also the organist of St Auban Cathedral. He and his assistant organist, Helmut Schumann, shared the duties and each played regularly at Moulins. They also gave regular recitals, often broadcast on French radio. M. Sarlat was booked for the wedding. The Curé, Father Lafitte, a charming man, would officiate, and had no objection whatsoever to marrying a Jewish bridegroom to a Catholic bride.

The guest list was straightforward with two exceptions. Lionel was very keen for his Gipsy friends to attend. They were the parents of his great friend, Marcel: Pavel and Irena Novak. Sandrine stressed how hard it was for Gaston to change his view about Jews. Gipsies would have been a bridge too far for the Leclerc family. Lionel said with deep feeling, "They are very respectable people, who have settled in Lyon for years, and have never been involved in any crime or caused any nuisance to anyone. I feel an affinity with the

Romani people, as many of them were exterminated by Hitler, along with the Jews and disabled persons."

Lionel did not give up on the argument, even though he saw that Marielle's sympathies were with her mum.

When Lionel got back to Lyon, the problem resolved itself. He went to the camp and met up with Pavel and Irena, who were in the process of packing up. If Lionel had continued reading the local newspaper, rather than planning for his wedding, he would have seen that the camp was in an area designated as a new retail park. Pavel told him that there had been fair negotiations with the Gipsies, who had received generous compensation to leave the site and find alternative locations in or near the city.

Pavel explained, "We have decided to move on to Austria where many of our wider family now live, including Aunt Rose."

When told of the wedding, Pavel was delighted that Lionel was to marry his sweetheart, but said that he and Irena would send their best wishes, but would not be able to attend. That resolved the problem, but Lionel knew that Pavel was being diplomatic, as he realised that their presence would have caused embarrassment on a special day for the young couple.

The other issue was what to do about Gaston's dad, who had always been so anti-Semitic. It was even more complicated because he was recovering from a mild stroke and was advised to avoid stress of any kind.

Gaston went to see his dad, as he often did on a Sunday. His dad, Gustave, looked well, although as a result of the stroke, he was unsteady on his feet.

Gaston embraced his dad and told him of the engagement and the wedding.

"Dad, I have decided to give my blessing to the marriage. Lionel is a fine and hard-working young man, who will love and care for my beautiful daughter. I cannot stand in the way of their happiness, and I feel that not all Jews are bad. There is good and bad in all nations and people, and Lionel is a good man."

Gustave replied, "I understand your point of view. I have loved Marielle dearly all my life. She was always so much nicer than her sisters, who were often so rude to me and Angelique. Marielle was always affectionate and respectful. I remember how she used to sit on my knee and smile at me while stroking my beard. Now I am old and may not have long to live. I do not want to harbour resentment, but to try to make the world a bit happier, if I can. I would like to attend Marielle's wedding. There is also another reason why I wish to attend, but I will not tell you about that just yet."

Father and son embraced, but Gaston was intrigued by the last cryptic remark from his dad. They also talked about the regiment.

Gustave said, "In a regiment, there has to be a common purpose and everyone has to be of the same mind, particularly in war. We need to agree on our friends and enemies. We could not believe that the regiment was wrong and that Dreyfus was right. The good of the regiment trumped all else. In peacetime, as now, things are different. We have to accept the truth even if it is unpalatable. I know that Dreyfus was innocent and that the Jews are not our enemies. No reason now not to welcome Lionel into our family."

Gaston was surprised but delighted with his father's response. Perhaps the stroke and the awareness of his mortality had made him rethink about what matters in life.

So the guest list could then be finalised. There were many Leclerc relations mainly from the local area. There were Sandrine's family from the South of France: less people on the Steinfeld side. Lionel's uncle in the USA was not able to attend, but there were second cousins from Zurich who were keen to come and meet Lionel and his bride but also Martha, whom they had not seen for years. Some people from Lionel's firm would attend, including Lionel's boss, M. Dupont. Apart from wanting to be at the wedding, he was fascinated to look at the site of the Midnight Train, now part of the folklore of Mallet Frères.

Many local people were invited, including Antoinette, the niece of Amédée, for whom she was still in mourning, and the curator of the museum, who had found the watch.

Chapter Eighteen

Much time and effort was devoted to choosing the bridal gown and the outfits for the family members. Stephanie and Véro would act as witnesses along with Rebecca, Lionel's sister and André, Lionel's best friend and colleague from Dijon.

Sandrine was in her element thinking about and preparing for the wedding. She went to Paris for her outfit, but also made regular visits to the new boutique in St Auban for accessories.

One day in April, Sandrine went into St Auban on her own by bus, and, when she returned and saw her husband, he asked her whether she had had a good shopping trip.

She replied, "Gaston, my love, I have not been shopping this time but I have been to see Dr Verger."

"Have you not been feeling well?"

"Not exactly, I'm pregnant."

Gaston nearly fell over at this most unexpected news.

"How can this be? I can't believe it!"

"It happened in the normal way. A man and woman have sex and sometimes the woman gets pregnant. This has been going on throughout history. We have been going at it quite well since we had that talk about anti-Semitism and Marielle and Lionel. All this talk of weddings may have got my hormones going."

Gaston listened, still amazed. He interjected rather tactlessly, "We didn't take precautions, since I thought you were too old."

"Thanks for that. But I am obviously still a young woman. We had a good time. It was like the old days, no longer lying in bed and worrying about the business, but doing what men and women are best at. If the price is pregnancy, I am more than happy."

"So am I, darling. But I am concerned that pregnancy at your age might carry some risk."

"Dr Verger said that I would be regularly monitored at the hospital and that there is no reason for concern, as many of his patients at my age have had successful pregnancies. I think it is wonderful that I am expecting. Apart from anything else, it will take my mind off losing Marielle and worrying about her."

"Sandrine, darling. I too am delighted. A new child at our time of life will lighten up our lives. I feel that you will need to take plenty of rest. I am quite pleased that I can still perform."

"Yes, mister, you still have lead in your pencil!"

Chapter Nineteen

Early in May, there was a meeting with the priest and the organist to discuss the details of the service, as far as necessary. It would be a normal Roman Catholic service, and the only discussion was about the choice of hymns and music for the service. The organist asked the family whether they had any preference for music at the service. None of the family had much knowledge of classical music for the organ. Lionel suggested something by Bach, which he had heard in some film. The organist, M. Sarlat, guessed correctly that it was the famous Toccata and Fugue in D minor, but did not sound enthusiastic. Marielle asked him whether he disliked that piece.

He replied, "No, it is a fine piece and I have played at many times. But it is not ideally suited for this organ, which has a vast range of stops and sounds and a much higher bellows pressure than at the time of J S Bach. I would have to hold the instrument back. It would be like driving a Ferrari at 40 kph."

They were all amused by this remark, especially Gaston, who was more familiar with fast cars than church organs.

M. Sarlat then suggested the bride should enter to the Wedding March by Mendelssohn. He played a few bars of this piece, which they all immediately recognised and liked.

He suggested that the Toccata from the Fifth Symphony by Widor would be a good voluntary for the end of the service. Again he played an extract, which sounded amazing. He pointed out the Widor had played that very piece himself on this organ. The priest asked about a piece for the Offertory. Without saying anything, M. Sarlat began playing a beautiful slow melody, with the sound of a plaintiff oboe above a soft and delicate flute backing. He told them that it was a Prelude by César Frank, who was yet another famous musician, who had played this organ.

The family were very pleased to agree to the suggested organ pieces and hymns.

As the big day approached, there were nerves and anxiety among some of the family members. Marielle was concerned that she should look her best and that there would be no mishaps with her outfit. Lionel knew that he would be expected to make a speech. Whilst he could speak with confidence about the merits of Mallet vacuum cleaners or AEG fan ovens, he was worried about expressing his joy at marrying his sweetheart in a sincere and meaningful way, and not messing up.

Gaston hoped that his father would not say something distasteful: he was aware that his dad had said that there was some other reason why he had decided to attend, but Gaston had no idea what that might be. Sandrine was worried about everything, particularly as to whether there might be any noticeable change in her figure, and whether her expensive dress might need any alteration. No one knew that she was pregnant apart from Gaston, and she did not wish to break the news until after the wedding: she was mildly embarrassed and also did not want to upstage her daughter on her special day.

Véro, however, had her suspicions. A colleague at the hospital thought she had seen Véro's mum going into the Obstetrics Department. Véro thought that, if it were true, maybe Sandrine went to get some sort of advice about birth control for Marielle. But why would Marielle not go there herself as she was often in St Auban? Véro put two and two together and happened on the right answer. She said nothing to anyone but when she met up with her mother gave her a sort of knowing look. Sandrine hoped that Véro would not ask her a direct question, and fortunately, that did not happen.

And so as the wedding day approached and guests started arriving. The first arrivals were second cousins of Lionel from Zurich, Eric and Joël Müller, who were related to Lionel from Martha's father. Eric was thirty-three and worked for a Swiss bank and Joël, who was thirty, was a civil engineer. They had driven all the way in Eric's Mercedes, a top-of-the-range model. They were handsome young men and smartly dressed. Eric indicated that after the wedding he was due to attend a business meeting in Strasbourg, something to do with the Common Market. Another second cousin from Switzerland, Verena, flew from Geneva to Paris and then travelled by train to St Auban, where Charles from the hotel collected her and brought her to Moulins. She was a hospital doctor, single and aged forty. There was a striking resemblance to Martha.

Large numbers of Sandrine's family made their way from Marseille and its surrounding area, as well as several of Lionel's people from Lyon. And, of course, André, Lionel's best friend, and his wife, Nicole. Rebecca made her own way to Moulins from Toulouse.

Chapter Twenty

There was a short civil marriage ceremony at the Town Hall attended by the couple, the witnesses and a few close relatives and shortly afterwards the church service was held.

The weather on the wedding day was fine and sunny but not too hot. The church service could not have gone better. The ancient Romanesque church was a wonderful place for this happy event, particularly in the early summer sunlight. The sound of the fine organ expertly played impressed and moved the congregation. There was a timelessness about the church; one might have sensed how many marriage ceremonies must have been performed there over the centuries. Even the more agnostic of those present felt something hard to describe; perhaps a spiritual feeling and a sense of the eternal. The bride and groom were indeed a beautiful couple, and Father Lafitte spoke his lines in a way which caught the mood of the occasion. Lionel and Marielle knew that they were man and wife at the end of the civil ceremony, but after the church ceremony, they felt joined in a much deeper and more permanent way. Many of those present in the church were moved by the ceremony and the sight of the young couple. A few tears were shed, particularly by those who had known the bride or groom since their childhood.

Amelie from Lyon, Esther's friend, was very tearful, and her dutiful husband, Albert, had to lend her his large handkerchief. She was thinking of Lionel as a small sad boy, now turned into a handsome bridegroom, but also of her dear friend, Esther, who was not there to enjoy the occasion. Too much emotion for her.

The reception was a most happy and relaxed occasion. The hotel staff performed their roles with all the precision that was the hallmark of Gaston and Sandrine's hotel. In view of the number of guests, there was a large marquee in the garden in addition to the usual hotel facilities. The hotel car park was soon full, but there was ample on-street parking for everyone who needed it.

Some speeches were made in the marquee and the crowd gathered to hear them. But everything was very informal. Gaston began by welcoming everyone to the celebration and encouraging them to have a good time. An excellent five-course meal awaited them and later there would be dancing. He spoke in warm terms about his wife and daughters and said how pleased he was to have Lionel as a member of his family. He made very friendly comments about Martha and Rebecca. He said that Marielle would be well looked after by Lionel and his family and friends in Lyon.

Lionel felt the need to say a few words, which in the event came to him easily. He expressed his love for Marielle and said that he felt he was a very lucky man. He expressed his gratitude and love for his mother and his grandmother, who had brought him up. He expressed his appreciation of and respect for Gaston and Sandrine, for their lovely daughters and for their fine hotel. He said that he would love and care for Marielle for all the days of his life. When he finished, there was a tear in Marielle's eye and a round of applause for Lionel's very sincere words.

But someone else asked if he could speak. It was Gustave Leclerc, Gaston's elderly father. Everyone wondered what he was going to say: hopefully not his well-known opinions about the Jews. He was a little unsteady on his feet, Véro took care of him and stood next to him. He began by saying how very happy he was to be there that day.

"Marielle is the most wonderful girl that I have loved all my life. She reminds me so much of her mother Sandrine, who came over to us after the last terrible war and brought so much joy to us. Lionel is so fortunate to have found such a bride, but she is fortunate too as Lionel is a splendid young man, who will make a wonderful husband. Apart from everything else, she will never be short of the best domestic appliances."

There were a few polite laughs and a feeling of relief, but what was coming next?

"One thing I am so sad about is that Lionel's grandmother, Mme Esther Steinfeld, is not here today. I would love to have met her. I say this for two reasons, firstly that I understand that it was she who felt that Lionel should come to our part of France. She must have felt something more than just a place to sell electrical equipment. She was not to know that he would meet Marielle and come to Moulins. She did not know that her dear husband died in that terrible train crash, but she passed away knowing the truth. Maybe she suspected something about our village anyway.

"What nobody knew was that I was in Belgium at that time in 1918 and was due to return to Paris – on that very train. I caught the Spanish flu, as it was called, and was seriously ill and kept behind in a sick bay. If I had caught that train, it is likely that the happy and lovely couple here today would have had two grandfathers killed in that same awful accident. Sadly Jacob's life was cut short, but mine continues into old age. I hope that I have spent my life in kindness and charity, but I fear I have not. Jacob fought bravely for France and was awarded with a gallantry medal. I did my best for my country, but I believe that he was a braver soldier than I was. Death and war take all alike whatever their race or creed.

"I am also sorry that Amédée Fontaine is not here to see Lionel and Marielle as man and wife. He was a wonderful and kind man, so intelligent and knowledgeable but able to talk to people like me as if I was his equal. It is good to see Antoinette here, also such a good and lovely person."

After he stopped, Véro hugged her grandfather and took him down to a seat in the marquee. There was no applause, his speech was too moving for that, but there was a sense of respect and empathy beyond words or applause.

After the shock of that expected statement, things grew quiet. Martha, Lionel, Gaston and Sandrine were particularly moved and were all close to tears. Gradually, the atmosphere returned to where it had been and the fun resumed. Not that Gustave had caused sadness, far from it, but his story had made everyone think about what really matters and what does not.

Gaston went to see that old man to comfort him and to let him know how moved they all were by what he had to say, which had remained secret for over fifty years.

All sorts of interesting conversations then resumed between people who were meeting for the first time in many years and also for those meeting for the very first time.

Martha had a long chat with Sandrine and her twin daughters. They expressed sympathy for Martha's terrible experiences in the war and appreciation for the way in which she had rebuilt their lives at Lyon. Martha expressed her genuine admiration for the hotel, of which Sandrine and her husband could feel justly proud. Then the bride joined them and was greeted warmly by Martha, who went on to speak tenderly to her, with the others present.

"It will be a big move for you, Marielle dear, to settle in Lyon, a large city far from your family, but it is a friendly place and I feel sure you will make friends there. There will be times when Lionel will be away on business trips and also when at home he sometimes works long hours. Remember, if ever you feel at all lonely and need company, I will always be there for you, with my family and friends. We both like dressmaking, although I am now a bit rusty at it. I have a good sewing machine and plenty of patterns. You could show me some more modern styles and techniques. We both like cooking and we could make some dishes together. I might show you some Jewish recipes. There's also the tennis club nearby, with indoor and outdoor courts. Lionel is still a member."

Marielle smiled warmly and looked much moved by these remarks. Sandrine had tears in her eyes and said to Marielle, "You are fortunate to have such a lovely mother-in-law."

She was reminded of her move to Moulins when she was a young bride and how kindly Gaston's parents had cared for her. This thought brought another tear to her eyes, particularly as Mum was no longer with them. She was sure that kindness would now be repaid in Lyon.

Martha then directed her remarks to Sandrine and her older daughters, "You are all welcome to come and stay with me anytime. I have a large apartment in the city near the Presqu'île and the Rhone. My children have flown the nest and sadly my mother-in-law, Esther, passed away earlier this year. So I have plenty of spare room, and would enjoy your company."

Sandrine replied, "It is not easy for hoteliers to take a holiday, but Gaston is talking about us closing next year from early January up to Valentine's Day. I would love to come and visit you."

Without mentioning it, she thought of her pregnancy (which would soon become public knowledge) and this made the idea of a holiday in Lyon rather attractive. If there was anything to notice about the shape of her figure, no one seemed to have noticed anything and her haut couture dress fitted perfectly.

She continued her conversation with Martha, "I was very sad when I heard of your mother-in-law's death, particularly in view of the strange story of the midnight train. It was so touching that she discovered how her husband had died and that she was buried with his treasured watch. We now know that Gustave could have been killed on the same train. I was wondering if Lionel was predestined to come our way, meet Marielle, hear about the train crash and find out that his grandfather perished in that train. It seemed more than a coincidence that he was also here on the fiftieth anniversary of that terrible train crash. If Marielle had not been in the library that day and not had time to help Lionel, he would probably stayed at St Auban and never come to Moulins and never met Marielle. He would never have heard about the midnight train or found out about the train crash.

"Incidentally, I understand that the train crash was not reported in the papers at the time, as the Government had issued a prohibition. It would have been bad for morale at the end of the war and with the flu pandemic for news of the accidental death of so many soldiers to have been published. There was local knowledge about it, but Gaston and I were totally unaware of it, having moved here after the Second World War. Amédée, of course, knew about it and researched all the details."

Martha responded, "Fate was not always good to me but I believe that fate has been very kind to Lionel, both in learning the fate of his grandfather and, of course, in meeting your lovely daughter. As you have said, it was Esther who suggested that Lionel should make a trip as far as north-eastern France and perhaps go to Belgium. She was a very spiritual person, who prayed for her late husband every week at the synagogue and kept a little shrine to him in her room. Perhaps she had some intuition that Lionel needed to go there for something more than business affairs."

Sandrine agreed that perhaps all these events were something more than coincidence. Lionel, overhearing this conversation, could not help thinking of Aunt Rose and her uncanny prediction of his romance with Marielle. He had never told anyone about it, but later he would tell Marielle.

Véro had taken a liking for the second cousin Eric from Zurich, with his smart suit, his nice car, and his interesting account of his life and work in Zurich. He spoke good French but with an appealing Swiss-German accent, which made him sound rather clever to Véro. He also took a liking to Véro, perhaps because he had a soft spot for nurses, but also he really like her no-nonsense attitude and straight talking. He also noticed the adoring looks she was giving him. It was obvious that there was a chemistry between the two of them, which even Gaston noticed. He wondered in a whimsical way whether in due course he would have a second Jewish son-in-law. At least, a Swiss banker should not be short of money.

Then the group was joined by Lionel's sister, Rebecca, who announced that she had accepted an offer to work for NASA at the JPL in Pasadena, working on the design of space rockets and probes for a future mission to the outer planets. Gaston and Albert from Lyon both heard this news. Neither could really believe that a young woman, however clever, could actually be an engineer of any kind nor certainly be able to do rocket science. They were particularly amazed that a young French woman would be doing this type of work and in America.

Rebecca kept away from them and was able to have a sensible conversation with Joël, the other second cousin from Zurich, who readily appreciated just how clever she was. He explained that a lot of his work was at that time in the Gulf States on infrastructure projects. He rarely worked in Switzerland or other parts of Europe.

Stephanie was keen to talk to Rebecca as she had always wanted to work in the USA. She asked how Rebecca would manage with her English there. Rebecca replied that it helped that her mother was an English teacher and that they had always spoken some English at home to help with her language skills. She added that most of her work would consist of equations, graphs and calculations, with no words in English or French. Fortunately, maths and engineering are international.

Stephanie surprised her family by bringing Ferenc Halmi with her to the reception. He was originally from Hungary and had been in St Auban for about a year. He was a very talented chef, who had worked in Paris, London and New York, and was now the Head Chef at the Lion d'Or in St Auban, which he had transformed from a rather boring bistro into a smart modern restaurant.

Stephanie broke the news to her father that she and Pierre had broken up, as he was having an affair with another woman. Later they discovered that he had been arrested for drug dealing. Gaston was delighted that Stephanie had broken away from him. Gaston did not mind the idea of a good restaurant in St Auban. To try it out, he had made it his business to eat there and was very impressed but the style of cuisine was very different from his own. He felt sure that the two establishments could co-exist very well and might even help each other by encouraging the public to eat out more. Ferenc seemed a very likeable chap to Gaston, a massive improvement on Pierre.

When Sandrine and Martha were on their own in a quiet corner, Sandrine said, "I must tell you something rather amusing. Stephanie has always had bright ideas. She suggested to Gaston that from Halloween to 18th November each year, we should have a Ghost Train-themed dinner in the restaurant, which should be arranged like a dining car on a train. There would be amplified ghost noises and sounds of steam trains. The waiters would wear SNCF uniforms."

She added that Gaston was horrified almost beyond words. He said that of all her terrible ideas this was the worst and that diners came to his restaurant for good food and service, not for nasty gimmicks and pantomime.

He also added with intense feeling, "It would be most disrespectful to those who had died in the train crash. Was this something Pierre had put into your head?"

Sandrine and Martha both had a good laugh, and Martha said that she was pleased with the good taste of Gaston.

Sandrine with emotion in her voice whispered to Martha, "I am so happy for Marielle, but I shall really miss her. She has always been my baby, though I realise that she is perfectly grown up. I still love to do her hair, help her choose clothes and assist with her make-up. She has always had such a sweet nature."

Martha gave Sandrine a hug and said, "We will take great care of her."

After a sumptuous meal, lots of champagne and a massive croquembouche, there was a break and dancing followed in the evening, until after midnight.

The wedding had not only joined the couple in matrimony but also cemented the relationship between the two families. This was an important part of a wedding in France at that time.

Chapter Twenty-One

The next day the happy couple departed for an idyllic honeymoon in Corsica, a time for relaxation and intimacy. This was the first time that either of them had flown and there was a mixture of fear and excitement. When they landed at Ajaccio, there was relief and real excitement. A taxi took them to their hotel in the small village of Corgese, not far from Ajaccio. It was a small and simple hotel overlooking the harbour in the village. They received a very warm welcome from the proprietors Carlu and Catalina Luciani. They spoke good French but with a strong accent, which made the newlyweds feel as if they were in a foreign country; not an unpleasant feeling at all. Nothing was too much trouble for the Luciani and Lionel and Marielle had a wonderful honeymoon in Corgese.

Their marriage was consummated on their first night at the hotel. As they were both inexperienced, their love-making could have gone better on that first occasion. The next day they decided that perhaps they should read the book, which Véro had given them, "Advice for Newlyweds on Honeymoon". It was mainly about sex and how to do better, but also covered a range of other matters.

Apart from love-making, there were other nice things to do, such as boat trips from the harbour. One day, Carlu's brother, Stephanu, took them out in his fishing boat to catch bream. In those days before the widespread practice of gill-netting, bream and other quality fish were plentiful around the shores of the island. Most of the fish were caught in nets, as Stephanu was a professional fisherman, but he also taught his guests how to fish on rod and line, using prawn as bait.

Stephanu told them how to strike to ensure that the hook would catch the fish. Otherwise, it might just take the bait and swim away with a free meal. He explained that strike meant that you had to lift the tip of the rod firmly so that the line would be tight and the fish would not escape. Stephanu also advised that, with bream, it was necessary to strike on the first touch by the fish. Lionel was a slow learner, but Marielle managed to catch several good-size fish. Lionel got overenthusiastic at striking and could not tell the difference between the weight bouncing on the seabed and a touch by a fish. Marielle, however, seemed to have a sixth sense, and each time she struck, it was precise, and there was a fish on her line. She caught seven bream in quick succession, and Stephanu wondered about offering her a job. As a youngster, she had fished for trout with her dad, and striking was something in which she had experience. At sea and fishing for bream was, of course, very different, but in all fishing, there are certain core skills, and Marielle's experience helped her. She was pleased to have done well and to have impressed her host, but she really hoped that Lionel would catch a fish soon, as she did not want him to be disappointed. She encouraged him, by saying that she was just having beginner's luck.

Eventually, he caught the largest bream of the day, and he and Marielle were both delighted.

Near the end of the trip, Stephanu to his surprise caught a tuna of over 20 kilos. That made the trip very profitable for him and put tuna on the menu in many restaurants in the area.

There were also wonderful walks in the wild and remote heathland, but Carlu advised them not to stray too far from the village, as there might be bandits about and also some dangerous wild animals such as the sanglier. The young couple took due care and avoided any trouble. They found an area of pine wood, not far from the village and spent time there in the heat of the afternoon. It reminded them of their first day together at Moulins, when they went into the pine wood and Lionel first told Marielle that he was in love with her. They made love in the Corsican pinewood; such a location was not something mentioned in Véro's book, but they decided to give it a go anyway, without any ill effects.

The cuisine in the hotel was excellent: traditional Corsican dishes cooked using fresh local ingredients and cooked with care. Apart from the fresh local fish and shellfish, there were the traditional favourites such as veau aux olives and civet de sanglier. Carlu used to hunt for sanglier in his youth, but, having been attacked by one when he was young, he gave up hunting and elected to buy his wild boar from hunters or butchers. Lionel really enjoyed the sanglier but realised afterwards that it was the meat of a wild pig. His avoidance of pork was more cultural than religious, and he was not unduly concerned. Marielle suggested that the writers of the Old Testament did not have sanglier in mind, as there were probably none of them in Palestine in those days.

"Anyway," she joked, "they didn't speak French, and would not have known the word 'sanglier' to put in Leviticus."

Lionel was getting used to his wife's sense of humour but, contradicting her in the same vein, responded, "But everyone knows that French is God's first language!"

After their discussion about sanglier, they took an evening walk into the village centre. There was not much nightlife, in that quiet village. Sometimes, as on that particular evening, musicians would play folk or other traditional music in the village square. They enjoyed the songs sung so well in a Corsican dialect.

At other times, Lionel and Marielle were content to sit on the balcony and watch the sun setting over the Mediterranean. Lionel did not normally drink alcohol except on special occasions, but he enjoyed the champagne at the wedding reception and also sampled the local Corsican wine. Marielle found the Corsican wine very different from the wines served at the hotel in Moulins. Carlu explained that the grape varieties used were usually of Italian origin, which suited the Corsican climate better than the well-known French grapes. She particularly liked the Patrimonio wines. She would suggest to her dad that they should get some for the hotel. Lionel acquired a taste for chilled rosé wine from the island, although he drank very modestly.

There was plenty of lovely fresh fruit juice to choose from so that Lionel never needed to feel that he had lost out by avoiding alcohol.

Lionel also suggested that they should take back some Corsican recipes for use at the hotel in Moulins. Marielle was not sure that this would work, as the Corsican cuisine was dependent on the local fresh ingredients, especially excellent fish, fresh herbs and olives. Gaston always looked for ingredients local to his environment.

During the honeymoon, Marielle broke the news to Lionel that her mother was pregnant. Lionel's reaction was the same as that of Gaston.

Surely she is too old, he thought but was too polite to say so.

Marielle now knew him well enough to read his thoughts and said, "It came as a complete surprise, and Dad said that he thought she was too old to get pregnant. But he was delighted with the news, just like Mum. Perhaps it will be the boy he has always wanted. It will be due in late January. I hope it will all go well."

"It will be odd for you to have a brother or sister so much younger than you. It will be strange for me to be the brother-in-law of a baby, but it should be fun."

"As Mum is expecting, it makes it more likely that she will come and see us in Lyon, as she will have to ease off in the hotel before long."

"I guess so. That would be lovely. Your mum is great and she gets on well with mine too."

As it seemed a good time to tell his secret story, Lionel also told Marielle all about Aunt Rose and her foretelling of his love affair and marriage to her.

"I did not believe in that sort of thing, but she was so charismatic and convincing that I ended up taking her seriously. After I fell in love with you, Marielle darling, it dawned on me that you perfectly fitted the girl whom she had described to me all those years ago. She even predicted that we would have a problem and that it would be resolved. It's uncanny. She also said that I would do well in my career."

"I don't believe in fortune-tellers, but your story is indeed uncanny. Perhaps she is also right about your career prospects. You are very good at your job. I am aware that you are very fond of that Romani family, but sadly they have moved on."

After three weeks, it was time to leave and fly back to France, this time to Lyon Airport. They said their farewells to Carlu and Catalina, who expressed the hope that they would return for a holiday very soon. The young couple thanked them sincerely for their welcome and all the care they had received and said that they would love to come back to that beautiful village.

Chapter Twenty-Two

The couple had already secured a comfortable three-bedroom apartment, on the east side of the Rhone, within walking distance of Martha's home. They were able to move straight in, as they had already furnished it. While they were on honeymoon, Martha and Rebecca had aired it and checked that it was all ready for occupation.

The apartment was fitted out with all the latest electrical equipment, thanks to Lionel's expertise. He was only too happy to explain to his wife how it all worked. This was hardly necessary for a young woman who had spent much of her youth helping in a busy commercial kitchen and was very familiar with fridges, freezers, food mixers, juicers, cookers, deep fryers and vacuum cleaners. But love was young and the relationship was not at the stage when irritation can set in. She accepted his advice with the same affection as that with which he gave it.

Life was strange for Marielle when Lionel went back to work. She was alone for the first time in her life and in a city which she did not know. But soon things changed. Martha showed her great affection and gave her comfort when she needed it. Marielle got a part-time job coaching young players in the tennis club and made friends in that role. In the autumn, however, she found out that she too was pregnant, which Lionel was delighted about. Marielle had hoped to start a family later in their marriage, to have time to do other things, while she was young. In ante-natal classes at Lyon Hospital, she met other young expectant mothers and made friends with some of them. Her mother and sisters also visited her, and she and Sandrine had many discussions about childbirth.

Sandrine was well ahead of Marielle in the pregnancy stakes. Her child was born on 26th January 1970 at St Auban Hospital. It was a boy (at last). Mother and child were both very well. Gaston was delighted. They called the baby, Gustave Filipe, after his two grandfathers, Sandrine's dad having a name derived from his Spanish family.

Marielle's baby was born on 14th July (Bastille Day!), and happily mother and child were both well. Again it was a boy and they named him after his two grandfathers, Gaston Joseph.

Gaston expressed his delight and added, "You wait over twenty years for a boy and then two arrive in quick succession."

Lionel and Marielle had two more children: a girl, Véronique named after Véro, and a boy Marcel, named after Lionel's childhood friend, who sadly died. They would have liked to have more children, but it became necessary for Marielle to have a hysterectomy, which ended her prospects of any more children. The operation was successful and she had no more health problems.

Lionel's career went from strength to strength, and in 1977, he became the Finance Director of the company and also a holder of company shares. Aunt Rose was quite right about his career, so far at least.

There was one unpleasant incident in his professional life when Lionel had to fire an employee, Roger Toussaint, who had embezzled some of the company's money. It was a clever fraud, and Lionel and his team had to work hard to detect and catch the perpetrator, who was not only sacked but also served a prison sentence.

In prison, this man shared a cell with a serial shoplifter, who was also a neo-Nazi, but this inmate was usually quite discrete about his views and kept under the radar. He went under the name of Heinz, which was not his real name. Heinz stressed that the man who had fired Roger was a Jew. It was obvious from his name, and he was rich, which was a clear sign of Jewishness, according to Heinz. Roger began to link his grievance towards Lionel with a dislike of all Jews. The two convicts, (both of whom were innocent and wrongly convicted, according to them) were released on parole at about the same time. They joined a neo-Nazi anti-Semitic group, based in Lyon. The group talked about attacking Lionel and his family but decided it was too risky. There was too much good security at Mallet Frères and they assumed that the same would apply at Lionel's apartment block. They were not assassins anyway but just wanted to cause distress and fear. They discussed other options intended to be as nasty as possible.

One night in 1979 Lionel, who normally slept soundly, had a rather disturbed night. He had a dream about the train crash at Moulins in 1918. He awoke perspiring and Marielle asked whether he was having a nightmare.

"I guess so. It was about that train crash all those years ago. I kept seeing those old photos of my grandfather with his pocket watch, and my grandmother was crying and asking for help. It was as if I was paralysed, and could not answer her plea for help."

"It's just a dream, darling. We all get them sometimes. Try to go back to sleep. It's only four o'clock."

Lionel tried to get some more sleep but he felt uneasy.

When he came back from his work the next day, he was told the news that the Jewish Cemetery had been vandalised, with Nazi graffiti on many of the gravestones. It was even worse for him because the headstone on Esther Steinfeld's grave had been smashed into several pieces. Lionel, Marielle and Martha were desperately upset, particularly Martha, who could not stop crying (so unlike her). She had always regularly visited the grave and laid flowers there.

"Can't these dreadful people even leave the dead to rest in peace? Hasn't Europe had enough of Hitler and his awful followers? Why did they pick on Esther's grave for the worst of the vandalism?"

This question caused Lionel to think carefully and wonder whether someone associated Esther's surname with him. The police were investigating, but there was virtually no security at the cemetery. There was a wall and a locked gate but it would not be hard to climb in. There had been no history of vandalism, and the Rabbi and senior members of the synagogue saw no reason for any more security. It was before the days of widespread CCTV cameras and of DNA testing. The police could only rely on traditional methods: e.g. did anyone witness anything suspicious at night? No fingerprints were found and there were too many footprints to be able to identify the culprits.

The cemetery was quite secluded and not overlooked by any residential properties. A witness came forward who had seen a van near the cemetery, but he could not give the vehicle's number, as it seemed it might have been covered over. The police checked hardware stores to try to find out whether anyone suspicious had been buying spray paint or sledgehammers. Nothing emerged from these enquiries.

Lionel tried to think of anyone who might have a grudge against him or his family. Suddenly, he remembered Toussaint, whom he had fired and who had been sent to prison. He went to see the investigating officer and passed on this information to him. It proved very fruitful as Toussaint and Heinz were out on parole. The prison authorities knew that these two were close friends and also knew their whereabouts, because of the parole conditions. When the police raided the apartment where the two were staying, they found paint spray cans, sledgehammers and wire cutters. They also found anti-Semitic material. Toussaint had an obvious injury to his hands and wrist, which was consistent with hitting a very hard object with a sledgehammer. The two men were arrested and the alibi which they put forward was soon demolished. They refused to give any information about other participants or the vehicle which had been seen. They were charged, convicted and sent back to prison. Unfortunately, the rest of the group was not found nor questioned by the police.

The imprisonment of the two cellmates was no great consolation for the Steinfeld family, especially Martha, who felt that she had been violated. Marielle did what she could to comfort her. Lionel provided a new headstone for the grave, and the family laid flowers there every few days. Lionel also made a substantial contribution for extra security at the cemetery, including barbed wire fencing, better gates and locks, and an up-to-date burglar alarm system, linked to the local police station. He was more than happy to pay but felt sad that such measures were necessary. He also felt it eerie that he should have had that nightmare at about the time when the vandalism took place. It was as if Jacob's watch (buried with Esther) was trying to tell him to help.

Martha had by this time retired from the lycée and was not in the best of health. She found it very hard to get over the vandalism which had occurred, which kept giving her a feeling of anxiety. Lionel was also concerned about the safety of his young family. They decided to take more care, especially if one of them was out after dark, in a secluded area. They were reassured by the support of their neighbours, who were horrified at what had happened in their peaceful city. There was a sort of neighbourhood watch arrangement, whereby the residents took note of any suspicious characters in the neighbourhood.

Martha's health gradually deteriorated, and it seemed that the trauma of the desecration of her mother's grave was an aggravating factor.

The desecration of the cemetery and especially Esther's grave, together with his dream of the train crash, made Lionel wonder whether there was more that he could do apart from helping to provide better security at the cemetery.

With his demanding job and the care for his young family, he had rarely, if ever, thought about the train crash and the strange dream which he had at Moulins in 1968. His recent dream had brought it back vividly to his mind.

Chapter Twenty-Three

There was a family get-together at Moulins in 1980. There was Gaston, Sandrine, the young Gustave, Lionel and Marielle and their three children, Rebecca, Martha and also Véro and Stephanie. Gaston's father was by then very elderly and in a nursing home.

After Lionel and Marielle's wedding, Véro had fallen madly in love with Eric, the second cousin from Zurich. The streetwise and hard-headed nurse had a whirlwind romance with the handsome Eric and they got married in Zurich. Sadly, it all went wrong, when she discovered that Eric was not gentle and loving like Lionel, but egotistic, controlling, obsessed with money and always in need of his own way. Divorce followed as soon as allowed under Swiss law. Véro remained in Switzerland for a while, working as a nurse in Lucerne. Marielle visited her there a few times to comfort her dear sister. They both loved Switzerland, its fine cities, its lakes and mountains and its ski resorts. They both enjoyed skiing and introduced Marielle's children to it at an early age. Later, Véro moved to Bruges, where she continued to work as a nurse, with the occasional love affairs but with no intention of another marriage.

Véro, who had made the short journey from Belgium, was delighted to meet up with her family, and they felt the same about her.

Stephanie, her twin sister, had married Ferenc, the talented chef from Hungary, who had moved on from the Lion d'Or to take on the post of the Head Chef at the Hotel du Centre at Moulins, following the departure of Martine, who, having gained a Michelin star, had moved to a top hotel in Paris. Ferenc would have liked to obtain a Michelin star and retain it for the hotel but that was not his main priority. He liked the approach of Gaston and Sandrine to produce good quality local food cooked in a traditional way. But he allowed himself to make changes to reflect his own background and experience. This went down well with Gaston and Sandrine. As for Stephanie, she had moved on from her rebellious period and settled down. She enjoyed helping with the business side of the hotel, at which she showed considerable acumen, to the extent that Gaston was, to his surprise, impressed with her. In time, the running of the hotel would pass to Ferenc and Stephanie with general oversight from Gaston. The hotel continued to prosper and later Gaston became Mayor of Moulins and had little time to devote to the restaurant. He also took seriously his role as a doting father of a growing boy, which took up much of his time.

At this family reunion, Lionel put forward his idea for a memorial for the soldiers who had perished in the train cash of 1918. He pointed out. "It was all kept quiet at the time, to avoid a loss of morale at the end of the Great War and during the flu pandemic. The soldiers' names would not even be included in war memorials in their own towns and villages, as they had not died in the war."

All agreed that a memorial for these brave men at Moulins was an excellent idea and Lionel said he was willing to pay for it or contribute if others wanted to help. It would include the names of all the soldiers known to have died, including Jacob Seinfeld. The proposal was put to the commune and was approved. Many local people were willing to make a contribution, including Antoinette, the niece of Amédée. She was now in a wheelchair and being looked after in a care home in St Auban, but she was still in full possession of her faculties. She was sure that Amédée would have approved of a memorial, and would not have seen it as a reminder of his father's tragic demise.

A fine memorial was erected near the Town Hall at Moulins and was unveiled on 18th November 1980, by the Mayor, in the presence of Lionel and his family as well as Antoinette. The event was also covered by the national media, who had got hold of the story of the midnight ghost train. The publicity led to an increase in tourists to Moulins, which was a benefit to the hotel. Fortunately, Stephanie did not revive the idea of a ghost train-themed night in the restaurant. She knew that Gaston and Ferenc would have vetoed it in no uncertain terms.

After the construction of the monument, it is believed that no one heard the midnight train at Moulins ever again: the dead could rest in peace and the inhabitants could sleep soundly.

Chapter Twenty-Four

Around about the time of the ceremony, Lionel met a business friend of Gaston, called Guy Lemaitre, a builder and property developer in the St Auban area. Lemaitre was not naturally likeable and Lionel saw him as a hard-headed businessman, with a streak of ruthlessness, but it was hard not to respect him, as he clearly knew what he was doing. Lemaitre mentioned the large developments which his company was undertaking, including a massive industrial estate on the outskirts of St Auban, where grants would be available for manufacturing industries, in preference to warehousing. Manufacturing created well-paid jobs, whereas warehousing meant few jobs and less well-paid ones; hence the former was favoured by public authorities at that time.

Guy Lemaitre made a strong impression on Lionel, who was a good judge of character. He felt that Lemaitre was a tough man, but was reliable and would deliver what he promised. Gaston expressed the same view to Lionel, who made checks on the financial status of Lemaitre's company, which showed that it was well-funded and profitable. Gaston and Lionel were also impressed by the developments being carried out by Lemaitre in the area. When back in Lyon, Lionel kept Lemaitre somewhere in the back of his mind.

Life for Lionel, the grandson of Esther, continued as before. As Aunt Rose had predicted, he was very successful in his career. He was excellent at his work and people liked and trusted him. This was true of the Mallet family, particularly in 1985 when he and the company were put to the test.

A new Paris-based company wanted to buy out Mallet Frères and offered a generous price for its shares. They called themselves Paris Mondiale, and it was well known that their business plan was to import cheap electrical goods from outside the European area, including the Far East and sell them in France and the rest of the Common Market at large profits.

Many of the shares in Mallet Frères were held by over twenty members of the Mallet family, most of whom were not involved with the business at all. The rest of the shares were held by the current directors, including, Lionel, the Finance Director, André, who was then the Sales Director, and M. Dupont, the Chief Executive. He was still called M. Dupont, but he had a first name, Alain, which no-one apart from his wife ever used, as he was so respected, and rightly so.

Of the two Mallet Frères (brothers) themselves, Jean-Pierre was by this time seriously ill and played no part in the management of the company. His brother, Auguste, had every confidence in Alain Dupont and did no more than keep a general oversight of the business, in his capacity as Chairman.

There was an underlying problem for Mallet Frères, which the hostile take-over bid from Paris had brought into sharp focus. Over the last few years, the world had changed and the company had not kept up-to-date. New cheaper products were coming onto the market from all sorts of countries, and Mallet Frères were being perceived as expensive and a bit too traditional. They were still doing well in the conservative home market, thanks to the efforts over the years of Lionel and his successors in the sales team. But they were nowhere in the export market: few outside France had heard about them. A change had to come.

The easy answer would be to sell out to Paris Mondiale and take the money, living comfortably thereafter. Lionel and M. Dupont, however, did their research and concluded that these smart men from Paris did not want their company as a going concern, but wished to close it down and sell its assets, including its valuable freehold site at Lyon, which had scope for residential development being near the new high-speed rail line. They and Auguste Mallet had a deep and maybe irrational affection for the products of the company, which they saw as part of French culture since the Second World War. They knew that their products were of high quality and would last for years, whereas the foreign products which they were seeing were inferior and not built to last.

They also thought of their employees, skilled engineers, designers, electricians, and sales and admin personnel, whose future would be in jeopardy, if they sold out their shares to a buyer who intended to asset-strip.

The three all knew that they needed a new business plan to provide a secure future for the company. They decided that they needed to modernise with a state-of-the-art manufacturing facility, producing high-quality electrical goods, with a made-in-France brand, but with scope for exports to all the countries in the Common Market, including the UK and Scandinavia, and maybe even to the USA.

They realised that they would need larger premises and wondered whether they might sell off their existing site at Lyon to fund in part their development plans on another site in the city area. Things did not work out as prices for real estate in their city and surrounding area increased with greater prosperity generally, plus the effect of the high-speed rail line between Paris and the South Coast.

The thought crossed their minds that they might need to relocate to a less expensive part of France, but this idea distressed Auguste, who was worried about any staff members who might have to relocate or become redundant. Many of their senior staff were, however, now near retirement, and might be happy to accept redundancy, if they did not want to relocate.

One night, in this period Marielle had a vivid dream, perhaps caused by conversations with Lionel about the takeover bid. She dreamt that Mallet Frères had a new factory near St Auban and that she, Lionel, and their children were living in Moulins. Unusually for her, she woke up in the night talking to herself and woke up Lionel, who asked her what was the matter. She told him what the dream was about, and he said, "It's just a dream. We all get them sometimes. Go back to sleep, darling. It's only four o'clock."

The dream was so vivid that, as much as she tried, she could not get back to sleep.

Over the next few days, there were long discussions between the directors of the company as to how to proceed. Following this, a general meeting of the shareholders was called, and Auguste Mallet, as Chairman, addressed the meeting, in his usual relaxed and confident manner,

"There comes a time in the life of every company when major decisions have to be taken. We are living in a changing world and need to face up to the challenges which it presents. There is the issue of cheaper goods coming in from the emerging economies, which threatens our share of the home market. Our excellent products are sold mainly in France, and we do virtually no exporting. We have not fully embraced the opportunities of the Common Market. We need to reassess where we are going, and I have been discussing this with your directors at length.

"As for the offer from Paris Mondiale (more like a threat than an offer: maybe an offer you can't refuse), we are strongly recommending you to reject it.

"Our researches show that these people do not want our company as a going concern, but want to asset strip. They are more interested in our site here in Lyon, which they would sell for redevelopment. They would also like to take us out of the market so that they could replace our first-class French-made products with cheaper imports from abroad.

"We need to update our manufacturing facility to keep producing top-class equipment, and our directors also recommend increasing production in the commercial kitchen category, which is very profitable, and not well served by anyone else.

"To be brutally frank, our factory dating back to the 1950s is now not large enough to produce the range of goods we need. Your board recommend that the plan should be to retain our premises in Lyon but only as a depot for the quality goods we import from our partners in Germany and Italy. We need to invest in a new manufacturing facility on another site. The problem is that property values in our area are very high, partly due to the high-speed railway.

"I will now hand you over to the Finance Director, M. Lionel Steinfeld, who will explain the Board's plan for the provision of a new factory in northern France. Some of you will know about this proposal already and may have formed views about it. Over to you, M. Steinfeld."

"Ladies and Gentlemen, I have been with this company all my working life, and it means so much to me. It is like a family, and M. Dupont has always been my mentor and friend. M. Jean-Pierre and M. Auguste have always treated me as part of the family. But this hostile takeover bid is a warning call to us. Through my family connections in the area of St Auban in northeast France, I have had very preliminary conversations with the developer of a large new industrial estate on the edge of St Auban. There are substantial grants available for the development of manufacturing businesses on this estate both from local government and also from other sources. I have also had preliminary discussions with a bank based in Zurich, with which I have a family contact. A loan on favourable terms could be negotiated, if required, for a well-established company such as ours, for the provision of a new factory. Our shareholders could, of course, if they so wished, invest additional funds in the company to reduce the size of any loan needed, but that would be up to each shareholder, assuming, of course, that you go along with the ideas which I am putting to you.

"A move of our manufacturing facility to another part of France, including for our workforce, would be a major change. We have consulted the key members of staff, including our Chief Technical Officer, Marcel Raymonde, who has been a stalwart of the company for over 30 years. He would be happy to relocate to the proposed area, as his wife's family are from Strasbourg, and his eldest son works for the EEC in Brussels. He has made some enquiries about the availability of skilled workers in the area, and it seems that the signs are good. There is a long history of engineering in that part of France, and St Auban, although not having a University, has a highly acclaimed Polytechnic, producing well-trained engineers, electricians, designers, as well as administrators and salesmen. Our investigations indicate that many of our younger employees would be prepared to move. There is less enthusiasm with the older staff, but most could remain at our premises in Lyon and some may opt for retirement, on favourable terms. More detailed discussions are needed, but it seems that staffing issues can be resolved.

"I will pause now for questions, but basically I would be asking for approval in principle to the proposal, to be followed by detailed negotiations with all the parties involved."

M. Auguste asked whether there were any questions.

A second cousin, Mme Eva Mallet, whose husband had been one of the early workers in the company spoke,

"Whilst I do not disagree with anything which has been said, and I appreciate all the efforts which have been made by the board, it would suit me personally to accept the offer from Paris Mondiale, in view of my circumstances as a widow, and as you may know with my two handicapped children. The offer is more than generous, and I am in need of the cash, to be brutally frank."

M. Auguste responded with sympathy,

"The offer is made only on the basis that a majority of our shareholders agree to accept. There may be some shareholders who would wish to accept the offer, but if there is a strong majority in favour of rejecting it, I think that should be the end of the matter. But for any shareholder wishing to accept, I think that the other shareholders should offer to buy the shares of that person at the price offered by Paris Mondiale. This would need a separate discussion with the person wishing to sell and with those shareholders willing to buy out the shares.

"Eva, dear, and indeed anyone else in your position, Lionel and I would be only too happy to do our best to resolve matters with you."

"Thank you, Auguste. I shall be pleased to have further talks."

A question was asked about accommodation for staff at St Auban both during the transfer and in the longer term.

Lionel responded to this point,

"The plan would include the provision of an apartment block near the site for all our staff working at the site and their dependants for the interim period. The company would lease it from the developer and hand it back when no longer needed so that it could be let or sold on the open market. But we would secure it for however long it was needed. We would have to provide financial assistance for staff to relocate and find new homes in the area. There is much new residential development taking place close to the site, as well as more traditional properties in the city and surrounding towns and villages. These costs will be carefully assessed and built into the budget for the scheme, which we would bring to you."

The discussions continued for some hours, and numerous questions were raised and issues discussed. In the end, votes were taken, and the shareholders voted unanimously to reject the offer from Paris Mondiale and to agree in principle to the move to northeast France. It was also agreed to treat the matter as confidential as far as possible, so as to avoid any publicity which might jeopardise the scheme.

Chapter Twenty-Five

For the next few weeks, Lionel and his fellow directors were very busy in carrying out all the negotiations with the parties involved. Lawyers and external accountants were also intimately involved.

This brought together Lionel and his second cousin, Eric Muller, who was now the executive officer of the Bank of Zurich in charge of finance for businesses. It transpired that Eric was in the course of being divorced by his third wife. However bad he was as a husband, he was excellent at his professional work. Whilst giving Lionel no favours as to financial matters, he gave very helpful advice as to how to structure the deals involved to the best advantage to all concerned.

When the two met for a drink after one of the meetings, Eric said how sorry he was that things did not work out between him and Véro. He now appreciated how badly he had treated her and how he should have tried harder to make the marriage work. He said that Véro was so much nicer and kinder than his later wives, who had married him purely for his money, whereas he knew that Véro had married him for love.

Lionel and his mother-in-law, Sandrine, had a talk about Eric and what he had said about Véro. Sandrine said in a reflective way, "How ironic it was that Marielle, who was so young and trusting, fell for a man who was genuine and true, whereas Véro who was sceptical and streetwise fell for a guy who was self-obsessed and turned out to be an awful husband."

Lionel responded, "I think he has learned his lesson, having had two very difficult wives. He wishes that he had looked after Véro better. There is no way she would want him back."

This was a very stressful time for Lionel. The move to St Auban was a dramatic step for the company, and it was Lionel who had devised the plan and persuaded the company to go ahead with it. Lionel had always been very confident in his work at Mallet Frères, both as a salesman and then as Finance Director. Although not great at maths, he knew how to read a balance sheet and a profit-and-loss account. He could assess the profitability of each of the products of the company. He could examine bank accounts closely and keep track of cash flow. He was an expert on taxation, both corporate and individual as well as VAT. But promoting the transfer of the manufacturing base to a distant part of the country, and managing that project was a giant step for him. It was also part of the package that there had to be an export drive, which would be outside his experience or indeed that of other directors or managers in the company.

His anxiety showed at home, where he could become irritable and also lose concentration. When Marielle or one of the children said something to him, it seemed that he had not heard. He was just not himself.

Marielle knew full well what was on his mind, and decided to get him to talk about it. At first, he was reluctant even to admit that he was under stress, but Marielle persisted, in her sensible and gentle way. She had matured considerably with age and experience, including bringing up three children and working as a tennis coach. She still loved Lionel dearly, as she had from the time when they first met.

"I have every confidence in you, my love, and I want to share the problems with you. This is a big step and it is not surprising that you may be anxious; so am I. Would it help if we went through all the aspects of the projects as if they were pieces in a jigsaw puzzle? Shall we start with Lemaitre?"

Lionel was not sure that her approach would help but went along with it.

"Yes, Lemaitre is crucial. He must provide a fully serviced site and build the factory in accordance with the architect's plans. It must be designed and built to accommodate the machinery coming from Hamburg Industries. We also need the residential block."

"M. Lemaitre is a very well-established businessman in that whole region. My dad knows him well. He is very tough in business, but when he has done a deal, he always delivers. He also knows all the important people in the area in government and in the companies that provide services like gas and electricity. His son works with him. I can't remember his name, but Dad says he really is a chip off the old block, straight-talking and business-like. I have met Louise, his daughter, who is lovely, but she finds her dad bossy. He did not like her boyfriend, who was a small builder. This guy, who had worked for Lemaitre at one time, told Louise that her dad was a hard businessman. Louise replied that you could omit the word 'business'. He was a hard man, full stop. She often had to do battle with him."

"Yes, I think we can be confident with him. He will negotiate hard but when we have signed the deal he will deliver. He will also help with any problems with politicians or councils, and chase up infrastructure companies. Doing the deal will be the hard part. Once it is done, things will move rapidly."

Lionel was finding the talk with Marielle more helpful than he had thought. She was so full of common sense, and practicality. He continued, "I must ensure that the gear installed by Hamburg Industries will be precisely what we need. This depends partly on Marcel Raymonde's assessment."

"Well, Marcel Raymonde is very experienced and the German company are the top people in this field. Between them, won't they get things right?"

"I guess so, but I worry about it, as I don't understand all the issues in this area."

"Do you need to? The same matters would arise even if the new factory was to be built in Lyon. You cannot be expected to know all the technical details. Alain Dupont will also oversee this side of the project, and surely he has years of experience in technical stuff."

"You are right. I must leave it to the experts. But the finance is largely down to me. I need to know how much we can raise from the shareholders and how much we will need to pay to those who want to sell out. This is tricky."

"Surely, M. Auguste will help a lot, as he knows all the shareholders very well and will give you all the support you need."

"Yes, but it's all so uncertain just now. And then there is the bank; the Bank of Zurich and Eric Müller. Matters have been agreed upon in principle, including the 10% share that the bank will take in the company. This has been agreed by M. Auguste and M. Dupont."

"Although Eric was not much good as a husband, everyone speaks highly of his ability and expertise as a banker. He always struck me as a man of his word. If the bank wants shares in the company, isn't that a sure sign that they have confidence in the project? In addition, they are making a loan, if required. The bank must be keen to do the deal, surely?"

"I think you are right, and I also feel that Eric has integrity as a banker.

"Then there are all the discussions needed with staff, which will be led by Marie, the Personnel Officer, under M. Dupont's supervision. Two trade unions will be involved, and things could get difficult."

"You told me that Marie has always had a good relationship with the staff and the main union. Hopefully, the packages offered with be attractive enough for the staff, depending on individual circumstances."

"Yes, you are right again. I should trust other people to do what they are good at. But I do not know how to ensure that the export drive will go well. It is outside my experience and the same is true for the others in the company."

"I don't know the answer to that, but it comes later when the new factory is in production. I do recall from when I worked in the library that the Chamber of Commerce and the Department for Trade had experts to help businesses which wanted to export. Maybe the same thing still exists and perhaps there are consultants who can advise."

"You are right. I need to investigate all options, including branch offices in other countries, especially in the EEC."

"I hope our talk has helped you feel less stressed."

"Yes, it really has helped me to think of each part of the task separately, rather than worrying about the total size of what we are doing."

"That's good, because you know I care about you more than anything in this world. If ever you feel a lack of confidence, you might think that Esther would favour the move to St Auban, and would be keeping a watching eye over you. Remember Aunt Rose said you would succeed in business. She meant all the way through your career, not just your early days."

"Yes, I feel better and Esther and Aunt Rose will surely be on my side. Thank you for listening to me, and helping me think more clearly. If it's okay with you, I think I will take a shower now and have an early night."

"That's fine. I wouldn't mind an early night. I worked quite hard on tennis coaching all day, and I am not as young and fit as I was."

Lionel took a shower and then went to their bedroom in his bathrobe. He looked for his pyjamas, but could not find them.

"Where have I put my pyjamas?"

"I have hidden them away, as you will not need them for my plans for you."

He soon realised what she meant, as she removed his bathrobe and took him in her arms, having also removed her negligee. She pushed him down on the bed, and laid on top of him, tenderly caressing him.

"Making love is known to be good for men with stress, and I am starting your treatment."

They made love, which they had not done for a few weeks. It still had its magic for them, but afterwards, as they lay in each other's arms, Lionel thought of Sandrine and wondered in a thoughtless moment whether Marielle might also become pregnant at almost forty. He immediately remembered that his dear wife was not able to conceive.

Chapter Twenty-Six

Eventually, after much work by all concerned, and with much burning of the midnight oil, the legal documents were signed and the move to St Auban got underway. Things went very smoothly, except for one unexpected snag. A group of Gipsy travellers had got onto the site, with a large number of caravans. Lemaitre was furious and said he would remove them with his bulldozers. His son advised against any such action, in view of Human Rights legislation. He said that they should get an injunction from the court. Lionel happened to be with them at the time, and said, "Would it be okay if I went on the site and asked them to leave?"

"If you want to get beaten up, you can try, but we will stick around in case there is trouble. You will surely be wasting your time."

Lionel went onto the site, dressed casually and wearing rubber boots. Most of the group were called, Lee, but he asked whether there was anyone there called, Novak, maybe from Austria.

"Yes," was the reply. "Emile Novak is the leader of the group, and he is over there."

Lionel went over and met a very large middle-aged Gipsy gentleman and asked whether he knew Pavel and Irena Novak.

"Yes, they are my second cousins and are now permanently settled in Austria, near Saltzburg."

Lionel explained how his friendship with the Novak family arose, including the sad death of Marcel, which they knew all about. Emile was amazed by the whole story and the coincidence of Lionel being involved with the site.

Emile explained, "We were on our way to Normandy for a fair and had stopped on an authorised site in Belgium, but we were moved off suddenly, because of some road scheme. There is a site near Rheims, which we could get to in another day's travel. As it is you, Lionel, who is asking us to go, we will leave at 8.00 am tomorrow."

Lionel broke the news to Lemaitre, and the Gipsies keeping to their word, duly departed the next morning, having tidied the site, and left it free of any litter or waste.

Lemaitre was amazed and enquired whether Lionel could do any other sort of magic tricks. Lionel did not feel the need to tell him about his friendship with a Romani family, and the reason why the group had agreed so readily to leave. He thought to himself, *Let him think I have magic powers. Perhaps I do. After all, I heard the ghost train in 1968, in this very area!*

The new venture proved to be highly successful. Top-quality products were designed and manufactured at the new site, with the Made-in-France logo. With external expert help, exports to Belgium, the Netherlands, the UK, Germany and Scandinavia went very well, and the company also retained its prestigious place in the home market. Eventually, the partners in Germany and Italy ceased to use the warehouse at Lyon and made their own arrangements for exporting into France. Mallet Frères were able to sell off the Lyon site at a high price and pay a handsome dividend to its shareholders, including the Bank of Zurich. They were also able to pay off the bank loan.

Lionel and his family were very happy to live at Moulins, where the hotel was now run by Stephanie and Ferenc and had gained a much-deserved Michelin star. Lionel and his family made a nostalgic visit to Martinsville Lake over the border in Belgium. Unfortunately, things had changed over the intervening period. There was far more commercial development there, including several fast-food restaurants and the tranquillity of the lake was disturbed by the roar of motorboats pulling along water skiers. Even so, Lionel and Marielle felt a strong sense of nostalgia for the place where they had first got to know each other.

Sadly, Martha died soon after the move to St Auban, at the age of seventy-seven. She was much mourned and was laid to rest at the Jewish Cemetery in Lyon, next to Esther. Lionel and Marielle visited the graves regularly when they went to Lyon to see friends there. Rebecca was now married and living in California and continuing her work with NASA.

The company had been allowed to propose names for the two estate roads next to the factory. They decided to propose, Gustave Leclerc Road and Jacob Steinfeld Avenue, after the grandfathers of Lionel and Marielle. These names were also a reminder of the train crash and the events which had brought Lionel to St Auban in the first place. The city authority on being reminded of the history of the train crash and also the story of the ghost train readily agreed to the proposed names.

Lionel and Marielle also felt that the names were a memorial to Esther, who had directed Lionel there. At this time, the memorial at Moulins had a deep and thorough clean: it was attractive to tourists and to other visitors, but unfortunately also to the local pigeons, who found it a convenient toilet.

The grandson of Esther, once a shy and timid young boy, was now a very successful businessman with a much-loved family, and living in an area with so many happy memories for him. He came to believe that Esther had guided him there. His love affair and his business affairs had come to a happy ending.

The End